My Girlfriend is the Grim Reaper?!

This novel is entirely a work of fiction. The names, characters and incidents portrayed in it are the work of the author's imagination. Any resemblance to actual persons, living or dead, events or localities is entirely coincidental.

First edition

ISBN: 978-0-578-42891-8

Cover art by sateencat

*To my own girlfriend, without whom
all of this would've remained a far-off dream.
Never stop seeking to love.*

1

This is the story of how I died.

Well - died, came back to life, started dating the embodiment of death itself, kind-of sort-of exposed the entire world to an entire set of other worlds and mythical creatures no one never knew were actually real, before ultimately having to work with them to save it.

…

Maybe I should start from the beginning.

It all started on what should've been a day like any other – I had woken up to my alarm the same as always, shut it off three more times like always, and - at long last - dragged myself out of bed. The house was near-silent as I shuffled from room to room, save for the occasional dripping of a leaky pipe, or creaking of an old door's rusty hinges, preparing breakfast and cleaning myself up with as much enthusiasm as a late-riser can be expected to muster.

My parents had divorced a number of years ago, and quickly found jobs in some far flung places overseas. Neither of them were ever neglectful, but when it came to anything beyond the bare necessities, they were far from what one might consider "invested". Still, it was thanks to them that was I even still able to live here.

The house had been handed down through several generations, and carried it with a wealth of memories, from my great-great-great-grandparents all the way down to me. So when my parents planned to sell it before moving away, I volunteered to stay behind and look after it instead, at least until I was old enough to move out on my own. Although I argued at the time that I was doing this to keep the old home from falling into disrepair, deep down I knew it was more about not wanting to go to a new school in a new place.

Sure, there were only a few people I could really call my friends where I was living now, but there was no guarantee I'd even have *that* much luck going somewhere else. And while it could be lonely at times living alone, I quickly figured out how to take care of myself, picking up whatever cooking, cleaning, and (more often than not) repair skills were needed along the way.

If you'd asked me how I'd describe life at that point, I'm sure I would've said something along the lines of "comfortable normality" – there wasn't much new or exciting in each day, and that was perfectly fine by me.

Stumbling into the bathroom, I paused to look in the mirror – yep, still the same 18-year-old boy, still the same Yuu Risher. Shaggy dark brown hair, light olive skin, and a slight build – practically the definition of unremarkable. People sometimes commented on my eyes (which were an incongruous light blue, thanks to a family lineage that spanned a decent chunk of the globe), but that was about all that stood out, physically or otherwise. It was most likely because of that that I could ghost through each day, drawing minimal attention. I got passable grades in school, kept to myself unless someone had a question about the previous night's homework or something of that sort, and chose to spend most of my time curled up at home with a book. If it wasn't for the few friends I did have, I doubted I would utter a single word during the day.

That's not to say I disliked talking to or meeting other people – I just never felt the need to go out of my way to bother them. If they wanted to talk to me, that was great, but really - there was never any need to assume that was the case. They had their own lives to live, and I had mine.

A happy, boring contentedness.

After swiftly brushing my teeth, combing down the more unkempt parts of my hair, and taking note of a drafty window that needed to be tightened up later tonight, I ran out the door and made my way to school. It was a brisk fall morning, so all the other students walking to school were wrapped in jackets and coats of varying colors and styles. By the time I reached the gates, the mass of bodies looked almost like a moving mosaic, a multicolored tapestry constantly shifting and weaving and students went this way and that. I took my place in the chaotic herd and fought my way to my locker, where I threw in my extra things and prepared to start the morning in earnest, which, like all the others before it, unfolded without incident.

When the lunch bell rang, I meandered over to my usual corner in the classroom, where two other classmates were waiting. Since the majority of students tended to rush the cafeteria at this time, the three of us had agreed to pack our lunches instead and eat in the classroom, affording us a little bit of breathing room and precluding the need to shout over a hundred of our peers just to hold a conversation.

To my left was Jun Agee, above-average in height, looks, and smarts, and…my best friend since I was a little kid. Although he had a habit of digging too deep into other people's business, and had gotten us both into less-than-desirable situations on more than one occasion, I knew it was all because he cared. Whatever trouble he tended to leave in the wake of his meddling, he was as dependable and trustworthy as they came, and was always ready to back me up when I needed it most.

Jun leaned back, brushing aside a few strands of sandy blonde hair and taking quick bites of sandwich in between his usual inquiries and theories as to the day-to-day going-ons of the rest of the student body. Himeo Hataso, another student in the same year as us, continued to quietly eat while listening to Jun's energetic rambling, her long, black hair tied into a neat ponytail that she draped over her shoulder. Me and Jun had first met her in elementary school and - whether through fate or luck - found ourselves in the same classes year after year, gradually growing closer as a group. Where Jun leaned on inquisition, Himeo simply seemed to know when something was wrong, or if something important was about to happen – be it a sixth sense, or just her own sensitivity to those around her, she had earned an esteemed (and at times disconcerting) reputation for her uncanny perception.

"Yuu? You with us?" Jun waved a hand in front of me, snapping me out of these reflections.

"Uh, yeah," I mumbled. "What'd I miss?"

"We were asking if you were doing anything after school today – seems like it's been forever since the three of us actually walked home together. You in?"

Himeo smiled slightly and nodded in consensus. Walking home as a group had admittedly become a rare occurrence, considering she usually had student council duties to attend to, and Jun had to get to his part-time job at a nearby convenience store. I never had much to do after school myself, of course, so I usually wenthome alone.

"Yeah, that'd be nice."

I couldn't help but feel a little excited at the thought. It was nice to break up the monotony of the day every now and then, even if it was with something as small as this. After agreeing on a meetup spot, however, I noticed Himeo staring at me out of the corner of my eye.

"You alright?" I asked. "Something on my face? Or have you finally fallen for my dashing looks and roguish charms?"

I thought this might at least elicit a pity laugh, but Himeo didn't waver in the slightest, only allowing a small frown to form on her lips.

"It's probably nothing," she said at last. "Just make sure you stay safe today, ok?"

I gave a nervous laugh at her odd, if not foreboding, response, and figured it was best to try to reassure her.

"Always do, but you know how boring my life is – "

"That's for sure," Jun interjected.

I sighed and finished my thought. "It's not like I'm gonna drop dead all of the sudden or something. Don't worry about it."

In retrospect, maybe not the best choice of words.

The bell signaling the end of lunch and the next block of classes spurred us to wolf down the remainder of our lunches and gather up our belongings. While Himeo's premonitions typically had some validity to them, I decided not to dwell on it for very long – even if she was right more often than not, it wasn't like she was *actually* psychic or anything. Plus, what was I even supposed to do with such a nonspecific warning? Never leave the house or -

Ah.

Either way, I figured she was probably just concerned about when I was zoning out earlier, and left it at that. And, as expected, I made it through the remainder of the school day unharmed.

After classes were over, I went and waited by the school gate, any hypothetical future dangers far from my mind. The sun was already cresting towards the horizon, though there'd still be plenty of daylight to make our way home if we left soon. Even with the night creeping up on us earlier and earlier, I couldn't say I disliked being outside in this kind of weather – watching the leaves stir on the ground as the wind tucked into your nape always filled me with a happy kind of nostalgia. Some might call the dwindling warmth eerie or depressing, but I always found it comforting in a certain way, like I was closer to a dream I could never remember.

The sound of approaching footsteps would've normally alerted me to my friends' arrival, had Jun's impassioned speech on the merits of extended break time for students not tipped me off before they even came around the corner.

Given that he was well-aware of her position on the student council, Jun regularly used Himeo to sound off on all the ills he believed were plaguing the school. I'd say she was a victim of circumstance, or at least a captive audience by way of social obligation, were it not for the fact that she actually took his rambling with the utmost sincerity – in fact, I had a sneaking suspicion that this strange relationship had led to several changes over the last few years, such as the dress code being relaxed and a few extra minutes being added to lunch. They made an odd team, but one couldn't fault them for effectiveness, however roundabout the means.

I waved the pair over just as Jun seemed to have finished rambling – at least I'd personally be spared his political tirades for another day. Setting out toward our respective homes, we settled into a more casual rhythm of conversation, sharing our ups and downs from the day and talking about upcoming events.

"Do you guys have any plans for the Lunar Festival? Any special someone you wanna ask, maybe?" Jun nudged me in the side. "Hm hm hm?"

I pushed him away and shook my head. "Nah, you know me better than that – I'll probably stay in, maybe read a book or watch a movie, something like that. The crowds alone are more than I want to deal with, anyway."

Jun's shoulders sagged as he clicked his tongue in disappointment. "C'mon, you'll have plenty of time to be a boring old hermit when you're in your – " He paused, counting on his fingers. "30s, at least. Late 20s if we're really pushing it."

I softly elbowed Jun and walked past him.

"Look, you've gotta live a little, right? Put yourself out there! Nothing's going to happen if you don't go out and seize it for yourself!"

"Maybe I don't want – "

I stopped myself, realizing how pathetic what I was about to say really was, even for me.

"All I'm trying to say is, I'm ok with things the way they are. I don't need to go out to have fun."

Every year our school partnered with a bunch of local businesses to hold a big carnival for the community. I couldn't recall the exact origins, but I was pretty sure it had something to do with paying respect to a spirit of the moon that farmers used to pray to, or something like that. Technically the festival had its roots in local traditions, but over time it became more of a way for students to celebrate the approaching end of the semester, and for businesses to rake in a bit of extra cash during the slow season.

"But it's only once a year! A little social interaction won't kill you, right?"

Jun nodded toward Himeo, as she tapped a finger against her lips. "Considering we're all free, why don't we go together?"

"Hey hey hey!" Jun ran ahead, walking backwards so he could still face her. "It's fine if you can drag him out for once, but what about those of us who already have a date?"

"If that was the case, you would've already been bragging about it 5 weeks ago," Himeo answered plainly.

I never thought I could see a man's heart shatter and recover in such rapid succession, but Jun was a man of many talents.

"Well then, it's settled! We'll all go together – we can visit the shrines, check out the food stands, and even catch some fireworks."

"Alright, alright, I'll be there," I said, trying to shake Jun off as he threw his arm around me.

I really had no reason to decline the offer, and it did sound like it could be kinda fun. I remembered going to the festival every year as a kid, though after my parents moved away, I just sorta…stopped. It might be nice to finally go back again, especially with a group to pal around with. Plus, though I was loathe to admit it, maybe Jun had a point. I might've gotten so used to letting life pass me by, that I simply of stopped thinking about it. This could be a chance to start turning things around, to put myself out there, make a change for the better, and (unlikely as it was) maybe even meet someone special.

As I silently resolved to cast off this self-imposed social

isolation, the conversation continued on to this and that, deftly switching from one topic to another with only the barest connections. Time sped by while we chatted, and, before I knew it, we all were saying our goodbyes and going our separate ways. The street leading to my house was a fairly quiet one, extending out beyond the tucked-away neighborhood I lived in, so for some time I was left alone with just my thoughts and the sound of cars rumbling by in the distance. It was easy at times like this to feel like an observer separate from rest of the world, only watching all these other lives go on around me, totally oblivious to my presence.

But then - something different happened.

I noticed a short girl, maybe a year or two younger than me, dash past a low brick wall, some hulking figure following in short pursuit. Any other day and I probably would've let it go, assuming it was only my imagination, that what I saw was some trick of the light, and the girl running past was simply trying to rush home.

However, today was no ordinary day.

Today was the day I chose to do more – to *be* more – than that. I would act.

And so, before I had a chance to think it over any more, my legs started moving on their own, carrying me after the two and bringing me to the edge of a dilapidated yard set in front of the crumbling skeleton of an old, abandoned house. The girl had backed up into a corner where what used to be a porch met the remains of a garden wall, holding her bookbag in front of her like a makeshift shield as she tried to protect herself from whatever it was that had been chasing her.

With no time to lose and the more sensible and rational parts of my brain tuned out, I ran forward to try to get between the girl and (what I had to assume was) her attacker. However, as my feet pounded against the cracked ground, the figure swung around, revealing its horrifying nature.

Although it had the overall shape of a human, a human it most certainly was not – the creature rested on long, spindly legs, muscles and sinew intertwined into a grotesque spiral, with elongated hands and feet that ended in something more akin to claws than digits. Its skin (if one could call it skin) was a leathery black, with a distended jaw forming into a set of pointed teeth. Staring down that thing face-to-face, peering into its glassy white eyes, absent any pupils –

I froze.

I had never seen anything like that before. I would've never even believed something like that could exist, were I not looking directly at it. It was the kind of thing that was supposed to be the stuff of literal nightmares and urban legends, not standing in the middle of an otherwise sleepy suburban neighborhood.

I wanted to scream, but no sound would rise from my throat. I wanted to run away, but my feet stood firmly planted in place. All I could do was my brace myself as the creature dropped to all fours and charged forward.

I went tumbling to the ground as I felt the full weight of the creature's massive frame crash against me. I struggled to hold it back as it slashed and tore and snapped with relentless ferocity, though my already-meager strength was rapidly fading. With a sudden and final sharp pain, a set of talons drove through my chest, and the creature at last yielded. It returned to its feet and, resting on its haunches, leaned its snout close to my body, as if to inspect it. As the last of my energy seeped away and a tired numbness overtook me, it reared its head back, as if preparing to howl, and then…slowly trotted away.

For whatever reason, the creature appeared to have lost all interest in both me and the nearby girl. I thanked my good fortune that it didn't attack again, as I vaguely watched her crawl towards me, my vision going blurry. I thought I might've heard her call out at the very end, though I couldn't understand what it was that she was trying to say.

The world began to spin for a moment, and then –

Nothing.

2

When I finally came to some time later, I immediately realized three things: my entire body ached terribly, I had somehow made it back to my room, and there was a girl sitting at the foot of my bed.

As I rubbed the sleep out of my eyes, I debated whether or not I should try to go back to sleep, given that this was surely all a strange dream bleeding into my waking mind. Considering the last few rays of sunlight were streaming through the blinds, it seemed most likely that, feeling exhausted after school, I fell asleep as soon as I got home and simply forgot all about it.

Satisfied with this line of reasoning, I pulled the covers towards me and prepared to lie down again, when the girl jumped as she felt the sheets move out from beneath her.

"Oh, you're up! Thank goodness, I've never done this kind of thing before so I was worried it wouldn't work and then I didn't know what to do and so I was waiting here with you but I wasn't sure if I could do anything to help and when you weren't moving I got scared but I remembered what you promised so I knew you'd wake up and – "

As soon as she had noticed I was awake, the girl started talking a mile a minute, her words lacking any real coherence or meaning. Who was she? Where did she come from? And what was this about making a promise? And - perhaps most of all - *why was she in my house?*

I knew the longer I let her talk, the more questions I'd only have, so I tried my best to politely interrupt her rambling.

"Erm, not to be rude, but – who are you? And what are you doing in my room?"

The girl gasped and covered her hands with her mouth – if I wasn't so utterly baffled by the situation, I might've been able to properly appreciate how adorable she looked in that instant.

"I'm sorry, I'm sorry! You…you probably don't remember anything, do you?" She crawled forward, smiling sheepishly. "I guess taking a mortal from one realm to another was bound to do that, and since you've never done it before, or at least I don't think you have, I'm sure there's a lot to explain, but where should I begin? I want to explain but I don't want to scare you or confuse you and there's so much to talk about – "

And there she went again, off on another stream of consciousness totally distinct from my own. For whatever reason, I could only think about how her and Jun would make quite the conversational partners.

"For now –" I interjected during a brief window of opportunity. "Let's get one of the easy ones out of the way first. Who…exactly are you?"

The girl paused and took a deep breath, fiddling with her hair as she looked away in embarrassment. "Y-yeah, you're right – I'm, um, Death. Or – I guess an aspect of it."

For the first time since waking up, the room was completely silent.

"You're…Death?"

The girl nodded with an odd sense of cheeriness and assurance, as if this was an entirely normal claim to make.

"And that would make me…dead?"

"No no no! I mean – you were, but you're not now." She moved next to me and crossed her legs. "You're very much alive."

"Then, if what you're saying is true, why are you here? And how did – "

A vague image flashed through my mind, of being thrown to the ground and bleeding out.

"How did I get back here?"

"Oh, um, about that…" The girl trailed off, pulling a few strands of hair between her fingers again.

"I really don't remember anything, so, please – whatever you can tell me would help a lot."

Although I wasn't exactly buying in to her whole story, some part of me felt like I could trust her, even if she maybe had a looser grip on reality than I'd like. I assumed my best bet to figure out what was going on was to try to be gentle and kind, and not scare her off.

"I didn't exactly see what happened when you died," the girl said quietly, staring down at her lap. "All I know is that when I found you, you had a big hole in your chest, and there was blood all over."

I instinctively moved my hand over my chest as she said this, though the hole she mentioned was entirely absent. And yet, I could barely remember something attacking me, and getting stabbed there. I thought that was all just a nightmare, but maybe…?

"So if what you're saying is true - and I'm not saying it is - you stumbled across my dead body. Then what?"

"I first came to this world in order to guide your soul to the afterlife." The girl at last seemed to have calmed down, and began speaking with more confidence. "When humans die unexpectedly, their souls don't have time to prepare for the journey, so it's my job – or, um, was my job – to help lead them away so they don't get stuck wandering the mortal realm."

"Then you're saying you're…what, the Grim Reaper?"

She placed a finger to her lips and, after a moment of deliberation, nodded hesitantly. "I…think that's what you'd call me in the mortal realm. I don't know much about your world, so I'm not exactly sure."

The rational part of my brain understood that the things this girl was saying were all just stories, made-up fables used to explain parts of life that were otherwise difficult to understand or convey. However, the fact that she wasn't wavering in the slightest in her commitment to this professed identity continued to cast a shadow of doubt on the plain and simple world I'd come to be familiar with.

"Ok ok ok…" I muttered, rubbing my eyes. "Again, suppose this is all real and still not some incredibly vivid hallucination brought on by whatever happened earlier – shouldn't the Grim Reaper be a bit more…y'know, grim?"

The girl watched me, wide-eyed and with a soft smile ever-present on her lips. "What do you mean?"

I thought for a second. Was I really starting to take this seriously as well?

"Well…if you really are the Grim Reaper, shouldn't you have a hood, and scythe, and be all skeletal and dark and brooding and whatnot?"

She had skin, so far as I could see. No hood or cloak, either – just a simple charcoal dress, which fit her figure nicely and flowed out at the bottom over a pair of similarly-colored stockings. About the only "dark" part of her appearance was the color of her outfit, and her long, black hair, which was combed in such a way that her bangs hung over her right eye. Outside of that, the only potentially-supernatural thing about her was how freezing cold her body must be – I could feel an icy chill creeping onto my legs through the sheets as she sat next to (or, by this point, maybe more like on top of) me.

She giggled and shook her head. "I guess I can see why you'd get mixed up. It's not like anyone I've ever met is still alive…"

As she trailed off, she gave a weak, humorless laugh.

"But there are lots of others just like me, and – no, no, I don't think any of them look like what you said. Unless – oh!" She leaned forward, her eye shimmering with excitement. "Have you met any other spirits before? Is that what they looked like?"

"Spirit? I – no, I don't think I've met anyone like that." I felt ridiculous for playing along even to this point, but I was finding it harder and harder not to believe her claims (if only a little), given how earnestly she was sicking to them.

"Then I'm your first…" she murmured to herself, a faint blush bringing a hint of color to her ashen, pale cheeks. "Oh! But you mentioned something about a scythe too, right?" The girl snapped out of whatever brief daydream she had fallen into and brought her attention back to the topic at hand.

"Yeah, I did, but – " I peered around the room, looking for ant stray weapons that might've been left lying around while I was unconscious. "You don't have one, do you?"

"Mm, one second – "

The girl reached back and unfurled a white ribbon that had been tied in the middle of her hair. With one smooth motion she cracked the cloth like a whip, causing it to stiffen into a pole longer than herself and materialize a curved blade at the top.

"Here ya go!"

Once more, I was rendered dumbfounded – I had just seen, with my own two eyes, a ribbon transform - in a matter of seconds - into a scythe.

Maybe at this point I should've stopped questioning the impossibility of it all and accepted this as my new reality, but the vestiges of a normal life and my own inherent understanding of the world clung desperately to the notion that this was still all just a very strange, very vivid dream, and I was sure to wake up any second now.

With as easy a motion as she unfurled her bow, the girl loosened her grip on the scythe and it returned back to its original state. She sat up straight as she tied the ribbon back in her hair, looking at me expectantly – I suppose that was my cue to keep asking questions?

"Ok, ok – if I really did die like you said, and you really are the Grim Reaper, or Death, or whatever, then why am I not dead now, and you're still here?"

"That might need some explaining," she mumbled, looking to the side and tapping her fingers together. "Like I said before, since you died so suddenly, I was sent to recover your soul and guide you to the afterlife. Nothing seemed different from any other soul I'd taken care of at first, until I brought you to the Middle Place."

"The...Middle Place?"

The girl nodded. "Spirits like me aren't allowed to guide mortal souls all the way to their final resting place. We can only take them to a sort of...transition area, if that makes sense. The souls that are at peace with their death move on, and those that don't, well – don't."

"Then what was I like?"

"You?" The girl stifled a laugh as she turned back towards me. "I think you were more confused than anything. You kept asking all kinds of questions, and even wanted to know about...me."

She brushed her hand across the sheets, tracing the outline of my lap.

"That doesn't happen very often."

Watching her now, with the initial shock of finding her in my room finally wearing off, I could see that this girl was actually pretty cute. Her smile was warm and inviting, and although she had a mysterious presence, I genuinely felt at ease being near her. If what she was saying was true, then I guess it'd make sense that I tried to learn more about us meeting - though that still left the question as to why I couldn't remember any of this myself.

As if reading my thoughts, the girl continued. "It's rare that a mortal tries to talk to me. If they've made their peace, they move on with minimal assistance, and if not, they tend to be so distracted by their own plight that they lose sight of all else that's around them."

"It must get lonely like that."

The girl shrugged, her expression blank. "It's just the way things are. It's what I was made to do. At least, until I met you." She sidled up along my lap and placed a frigid hand against my cheek. "When I met you, for the first time I felt something different. For the first time, I felt...warm."

The girl gently wrapped her other hand around the back of my head and pulled me to her chest, my heart racing and cheeks burning at this sudden, intimate display. I quickly realized, however, that it was as she said – a tiny bit of warmth was struggling through to the surface, reverberating in time with an absent heartbeat.

The girl released my face and went on. "As I learned more and more about you, this feeling only continued to grow. I didn't, I-I don't understand what it is, or where it comes from, but I know I want to be close to you. I don't want to let you go."

I listened to her intently, an unknown tension building behind each word.

"When you were ready to depart, I asked if you wanted to return to the mortal realm - to your home - instead. You said yes, and so I also asked that you do one thing for me in return, and…"

"And…?"

"Andbemyboyfriend!" The girl let out the entire sentence in a single (admittedly impressive) outburst and turned away, covering her face with her hands.

"Boy…friend?" I repeated the word, understanding what it was but not comprehending what it meant. "Then that would make you…my girlfriend?"

The girl gave a small nod, peaking out behind her fingers.

"But…why?"

"I trust you." The girl pulled her hands away from her face and bowed her head. "Like I said, I only get this feeling when I'm around you, and I want you to teach me what it means. You said it was, um…" She furrowed her brow in concentration. "Love!"

"L-love?"

"Mhm, mhm~"

She leaned in close once more, allowing me to get a better look at her face – her lips were a dark grey, though rather than stand out, they simply complemented the rest of her faint tone. Her eyes (or the one eye I could see, at least) were like a smoky wisp, the colors of the iris seeming to almost move and shift as I gazed at it. She certainly looked different from any "normal" human I'd met before, but that somehow only served to enhance her immediate charm.

"I'm not sure you picked the right guy for the job, though. I've never even been on a date before, let alone fallen in love. I don't know if I'll be able to teach you that much after a–"

"Then we'll learn together!" The girl grabbed my hand and held tight. "I know it might be a lot to ask, but will you still stay with me? At...at least until I understand what this feeling means."

"You did save my life – " At this point, all I could do was give in to the absurdity of the situation and accept it. "And even if I don't remember it, a promise *is* a promise. So..."

I glanced up at the ceiling awkwardly, unsure how to proceed.

"Will you...go out with me?"

The girl laughed softly and nodded. "Of course I will, I would like that very, very much."

I knew it was a bit redundant to ask after the fact, but I felt like I should at least try to do things "right". Still there was one lingering problem –

"But now that you're here, how do we exactly...date? I mean, you said you're not even from this world, right?"

"Oh! While it's true that spirits like me only get to see the mortal realm when a soul needs to be escorted, there is one way for us to stay here indefinitely."

"Please tell me it doesn't involve a human sacrifice or blood oath or – "

The girl rolled her eyes and smiled sardonically. "No, no, nothing like that. To stay in this world, a spirit needs to make some type of agreement with a human. So when you said you would be my boyfriend, that sealed our contract. To make it work, both have to offer something – the spirit gives up their position and lends some of their power, and the human gives up a part of their soul."

"Wait wait wait, I thought you just said it didn't – "

"It's fine, it's fine!" The girl waved her hands frantically, cutting me off. "The little bit you give up is so small that you won't even notice it's missing."

"Oh, well I guess that's fine then, so long as – "

"There's one other thing you should know, though," she added meekly. "If a human's soul grows too weak, they'll die – for good. When that happens, their soul is too frail to escort to the afterlife, and so they either remain stuck in the mortal realm, wandering between life and death, or, at worst, they simply…disappear."

My stomach dropped at this sudden and grave warning. Coming back to life didn't count for a whole lot if it ultimately ended in me fading from existence, or being trapped in some sort of endless purgatory here on Earth. My head felt like it was spinning as I tried to take it all in, when a brisk rush overtook me as the girl flung her arms around my neck in a chilling embrace.

"But I won't let that happen to you! You'll protect me, and I'll protect you – just like we promised."

I suppressed a shiver and awkwardly patted her back. "R-right."

I had to imagine this was in reference to yet another conversation I forgot about during my (presumably brief) tenure in the Middle Place.

"I should also let you know that there may have been a small…side effect from making a contract together." The girl pulled my collar down, exposing the top of my chest. "Any mortal that contracts with a spirit bears a mark of that agreement, holding some part of the spirit within it."

Peering down I was able to see that, sure enough, there was a simple design etched onto my skin – what looked like a triangle laid overtop of a circle.

"And, since you made a contract with a spirit of death you…can't really die now."

"I can't die?"

The girl shook her head quickly. "At least, not easily. You can still lose your soul like I said, and even if your body can withstand more grievous injuries than any other humans, you're not invincible. Plus, you can still feel pain, and – " The girl quickly amended her statement. "A-at least that's what I've been told. So you still have to promise to be careful, ok?"

She gave a sad smile, adding quietly, "For my sake."

The girl placed her hand against my chest, bringing to the surface a faint memory of a conversation not too dissimilar from this one. We were in a dark, lonely place, just the two of us, and she said…something about coming back here. About what it would cost? Or what I needed to do? Or…or…

Gone.

Like trying to recall the details of a surreal dream before it slips away, any recollection of that time with her faded away just as I was starting to grab onto it. All I could do was hope it'd come back to me again sometime later.

"I think I'm starting to understand," I said slowly. "But one thing's still bothering me."

"Hm?"

"Why can I remember so little about this? I know you said it's normal for people to lose some of their memories when leaving the afterlife – "

"Middle Place," the girl corrected.

"Oh, uh – yeah. What I don't understand is why I can't even remember how I died. I know I was walking home from school earlier, and I saw some girl getting chased, and then there was this stabbing pain, and then…then the rest is all a blur."

The girl frowned and brushed a few stray hairs away from my forehead. "From what I've seen, it's not uncommon for mortals to forget the cause of their own deaths – I think it's part of the process for them to let go and move on. If you take that with bringing you back to your world, and, well…you see the results."

I glanced around the room as a new thought crossed my mind. "Speaking of which, how did I end up back here?"

"Oh, when I brought you back to life you were still pretty out of it, but you had just enough energy to point me to where your house is. I brought you to your room and put you in bed, but since I don't know a lot about humans I couldn't do anything to help with your injuries, so I stayed nearby and waited for you to wake up, and I was worried that I might've done something wrong and you actually wouldn't wake up, so it was such a relief – "

"It's ok, it's ok," I said with a weak smile. "I wouldn't even be here in the first place if it wasn't for you, so you've done more than I could ever thank you for."

As I tried to readjust myself and sit up, a sharp, stabbing pain ran through every bit of my entire body – I guess she wasn't kidding when she said I'd still feel the effects of my injuries.

With few other options, I chose instead to put my hand over hers, which seemed to help put her at ease.

"Now that I think about it, I don't even know your name, do I? Unless, did I…did I forget that, too?"

"No no, you didn't! There's nothing for you to forget because I…don't…really…have one," the girl said softly. "B-but you're Yuu, right? You couldn't tell me your name when I came to visit you in the Middle Place, but I heard you mumble it once I brought you back to this realm, so I thought that might be it."

"Ah, yeah, it is."

One step forward, two steps back.

"Still, I'm gonna need something to call you as well." I thought for a moment. "Since tomorrow is Saturday, why don't we go on a date and see if we can find a name for you?"

"D-date?" The girl stared at me in complete awe, her eye brimming with barely-contained joy. It was hard to say that I wasn't being won over by her sheer sincerity and innocence alone.

"Sure, why not? That's what couples tend to do, um – don't they?" The girl shrugged and shook her head. "W-well, anyway, I'm sure there's lots to learn about each other, and plenty you want to find out about this world too, right?"

Although I didn't know it at the time, with that one, simple question, I had flung away the last remainder of what might be called a "normal" life, and dove head-first into a new adventure filled with spirits, monsters, and impossible romance.

"Yes, yes, definitely yes!"

"Then why don't we go down to the shopping district tomorrow afternoon and do a little exploring? I can show you a restaurant I like, we can check some stores, and - " I eyed the girl's dress – it was pretty, but there was no indication that she had brought anything else with her. "You probably only have the clothes you're wearing now, right?"

"Oh, this?" She smoothed out her skirt and pinched some of the material between her fingers. "Mhm, there's not a lot of need for material things where I'm from."

"Alright, let's plan on getting you some new clothes while we're at it."

"Y-you don't have to do so much for me, but…thank you."

Seeing her smile in my direction gave me butterflies like nothing else. Even if we'd only just met, I knew I wanted to hold on to that smile forever.

The girl stretched out next to me and laughed to herself. "Wearing clothes, eating food, going to sleep – there's a lot to think about living in the mortal realm, huh?"

"I guess – "

The mere mention of the word "sleep" forced an extended yawn out of me, as all the exhaustion that had been piling up finally caught up.

"I guess there is…" I murmured, as a gentle voice whispered in my ear:

"Goodnight, Yuu~"

3

I awoke the next morning to a strangely quiet room.

I made sure to always set an alarm every night, even on the weekends (though this was more in an effort to at least pretend I would get up at a normal time), so to not be greeted by a blaring and incessant beeping first thing in the morning was a bit out of the ordinary. As I sat up and tried to rub the last remnants of sleep from my eyes, I noticed the girl lying peacefully at my side, and all at once recollection came flooding back.

There was some kind of accident, I died, met Death, and now we were dating.

I still struggled to believe any of it was true, but the evidence was right in front of me – the scar on my chest, the hazy, half-formed memories from yesterday, and the girl who showed up out of nowhere knowing my name and having supernatural powers.

Of course, the novel circumstances didn't end there – I had never been in a relationship, let alone had a female "friend" spend the night, so I was at a loss with regard to the proper etiquette. Should I wait until she wakes up? Wake her up myself? Should I…touch her to do that? Where's an appropriate place? Is that moving too fast? Would she be offended if she woke up and I wasn't there, or would she think

I was weird for watching her while she was sleeping?

Seeing no end to this dizzying stream of questions, I gathered my resolve and settled on a plan of action that felt the most "boyfriend-like" (whatever that meant). If I was able to get out of bed without disturbing her, I could get cleaned up and cook breakfast, while still letting her continue to rest. It wasn't much, but I thought it might give a good first impression, and help her feel a little more welcome in my home.

Determined to start things off on the right foot, I slowly moved to the side of the bed, and –

No luck. The girl must've grabbed onto my shirt sometime during the night, and was holding on tight. I turned back to her and tried to carefully pry her fingers away, though to no avail – she had a vice-like grip, and no matter how much I tugged or shifted, her hand would not budge.

If being sneaky didn't work, then I'd just have to a direct approach. I placed my hands on her shoulder and shook gently.

"Hey, it's time to wake up – "

"Mmnh…warm~" the girl mumbled as she threw her other arm around me in an even tighter hold.

My options rapidly diminishing, there was only thing left to do – I'd have to tear myself away from the bed (and girl) in one go. I hoped that if I was fast enough, I might be able to do it without her even noticing, like when entertainers pull a tablecloth out from under a set of dishes without them falling. And so with one mighty leap, I threw myself from the bed and landed on the floor –

Followed shortly after by a resounding thud.

I quickly turned around to find the girl still clutched to my shirt, half of her body slumped over the bed and on the ground. It might've been a funny sight if I wasn't now terrified that I may have just concussed my girlfriend on the very first morning we spent together.

As I started to speculate if spirits even *could* suffer concussions, I knelt down and scooped the girl up in my arms (despite being only a few inches shorter than me, she was surprisingly light) and placed her back to the bed. She seemed to have barely stirred, even with her sudden tumble, her breathing steady and soft, the contented smile unwavering – I breathed a sigh of relief as it looked like she'd be ok for now. Plus, at some point during the previous scuffle, she had finally let go of my shirt, so at least I was now free to go about my morning routine.

Heading into the kitchen, I flicked on the radio and caught the tail end of a report detailing the ongoing vandalism "crisis" that was plaguing the city. There didn't seem to be any clear connection between all the cases, since the magnitude of damage was different each time – some buildings looked like they were torn apart from the inside out, while others only suffered a broken window or scratched door.

Given the lack of a clear pattern or motivation, everyone from news broadcasters to teachers to neighbors had been hurling out speculations as to the ultimate cause, though the local government held fast in its assurance that no one was in any real danger, and that investigations had already turned up some promising leads; considering what a regular occurrence these incidents had become, most people around me seemed to treat them with more fascination than fear. I suppose this was by the fact that the neighborhood I lived in hadn't been targeted yet, though even in places where the damage was most severe, life went on unabated. The human ability to adapt to any situation was both a useful and fascinating thing.

As I listened to the rest of the daily news, I went about

robotically preparing breakfast, just like every other morning for the past however many years. I had grown accustomed to only having to worry about myself, so when I stopped to think about it, I really had no idea how to take of another person. Or spirit.

"Come to think of, it do they even ea-a-a-t?!"

This line of thinking was abruptly cut off as a brisk chill ran across my back and an ethereal figure came fading through the wall. I let out a small yelp and dropped the pan I was holding, spilling its contents all over myself and the floor.

With a light yawn and rubbing her one exposed eye, the girl floated over to me, still half-asleep. "Hrm, Yuu? Is everything ok?"

Trying to catch my breath and settle my pounding heart, I muttered out a weak reply. "Y-yeah, all good. Just caught me off-guard, is all."

The girl opened her eye a bit wider when she realized what happened, and began rapidly bowing her head. "I'm sorry, I'm sorry, I'm sorry! I forgot you're probably not used to seeing a spirit in person, I-I didn't mean to startle you!"

As she continued on with a lengthy string of apologies, I saw that the girl was hovering just above the ground. Despite initial appearances, there still seemed to be plenty that set her apart from a regular human like me.

"It's ok, really. I just…didn't know you could do things like that, is all. If anything, it's kind of impressive."

This small compliment seemed to cheer her up, and she gave a timid smile. "I-I'm glad you don't think it's weird or anything."

"Well, sure it's…*different*, but everyone has unique things about them; I wouldn't say that's a bad thing by any means.

Though if we're gonna go out in public together, we should probably work on making sure you blend in."

The girl tilted her head, confused, so I tried to elaborate.

"I'm not sure if other people are ready to meet a ghost – "

"Spirit," she interrupted. "Ghosts are different."

"Uh, right. I'm not sure if people are ready to meet a spirit – "

A satisfied nod.

"Yet. I don't think everyone will be as accepting or understanding if they find out you're not really human, so let's try to work on acting as normal as possible."

"What do you mean?"

"Y'know…no floating through walls. Or in general."

"Sounds like you're just jealous," she said with a huff, turning her head away.

"Ok maybe just a little. But when we're out around other people, let's try to keep it to a minimum. Deal?"

The girl peeked in my direction and raised one eyebrow. "Will you do something for me too, then?"

"Sure, if it's something I actually can do."

She silently moved towards me and rested her chin against my chest. "You'll take me out on a date today, right?"

"Mhm, that's what I promised."

"Then…" She took a step back, and, with a dramatic turn, threw her hands up. "Let's make this the best date ever!"

"Alright, alright, I'll do my best," I said, laughing and shaking my head at the sudden change in atmosphere. Honestly, I had no idea what I should do on a normal date, let alone how I would make this one the "best" ever, but at least we weren't lacking for enthusiasm. Although there was still a slightly more pressing issue still splattered all over the floor.

"Also, I hate to say it, but it looks like I won't be able to make breakfast today." I brushed some of the residual batter off my shirt and nodded towards the doorway. "Why don't you go get cleaned up, and we'll get something to eat while we're out instead? The bathroom's upstairs, first door on the right."

The girl gave a quick thumbs up and cheerily drifted away, humming to herself.

...

Looks like I'd have my work cut out for me. At least she didn't go through the wall this time.

After scrubbing down the floor and freshening up as well, I met back up with the girl downstairs – she had on the same charcoal dress as before, the skirt fluttering out around her knees, and the white ribbon tied into a neat, loose bow in the middle of her dark black hair. I still couldn't understand how a supposed spirit of death could be this cute.

"So, are you hungry?" I paused. "You…do eat food, right?"

The girl tapped her chin, thinking it over. "Mm, normally I feast on the souls of the recently departed, but mortal food could be nice to try, too."

I waited for her to crack a smile or laugh, but none were forthcoming.

"Wait, you're – "

"Joking, yes." She shook her head in disappointment. "I already told you I help souls, not eat them, right?"

"Well, yeah, it's just – " I started to mumble. "I don't know anything about spirits, or how they live."

"I don't think we're all that different, honestly. Even if the spirits of each realm are all distinct in their own, taken together we're more human than you might assume." She glanced at me and smirked. "Which, now that I'm here, includes eating."

As if to accentuate this point, her stomach let out a low grumble.

"Ok, ok – let's find a place to eat at first, and then look for some new clothes. I'm not sure how long that one outfit will be able to last you."

I would've been happy to lend her some of my clothes, but our "proportions" differed in several key ways. Plus, I doubted she would be happy being stuck wearing plain jeans and t-shirts all the time; it'd be good for her to pick out her own wardrobe.

Looking back, it might seem absurd to have so easily welcomed a complete stranger into my home, but it wasn't like I had much of a choice – after all, where else could she go? I had thought about asking Himeo if she could stay with her instead, at least until I figured out a more permanent solution, but I had no clue how I'd even begin to explain the situation I'd stumbled into. Plus, it wasn't like I was hurting for space here. If my new girlfriend was happy to stay with me, I was happy to have her.

"Let's go, let's go!" the girl proclaimed, practically shoving me out the door. "Our first date, first date~" She skipped ahead while singing to herself, radiating a childlike exuberance that I had to admit was rubbing off on me as well.

"I have to warn you, I don't really know what I'm doing," I said with a half-smile. running to catch up with her.

As if in response, a fast-familiar chill overtook my arm. I glanced over to the girl as she swiftly withdrew her hand and held it close to her chest.

"I-I've seen other couples do this whenever I visited this world, so…so I wanted to try it too. Is that ok?"

I carefully reached out and took her hand back in mine,

locking our fingers together for the only reply she needed.

Even though the shopping district was only a short walk from my house, the girl somehow managed to come up with a seemingly endless number of questions about every single thing we passed by. She wanted to know what kinds of trees were lining the sidewalk, what kind of creatures the birds flying above were, why clouds were always moving like that, what that big bright ball in the sky was, where these people were going and who those people were, and what it's like to live in this place, and if I've ever gone anywhere else before, and where I want to go in the future, and how so many people live in such a small place, and –

Well, you get the idea.

Once we reached the central plaza and I started looking around for any place that might be good to stop in for a bite to eat, I caught a glimpse of the girl's face, aglow with infinite wonder. She turned towards me, mouth slightly agape, and exclaimed, "I've never seen the mortal realm like this! Th-there's smells, and sounds, and colors, and people, and animals everywhere, and – look, look over there!"

Without specifying what it is that had caught her attention now, she grabbed my hand and dragged me forward in some unknown direction, the excitement of it all having completely overtaken her.

A few minutes more of hectic wandering, and we at last stopped (or in my case, stumbled) in front of a bakery. My guess was that the smell of freshly-made bread and the light hint of spices had enticed her, which I couldn't fault her for – the shop was well-known, even outside the citym for not only its quality, but the sheer variety on offer.

"Do you want to in and eat?" I ventured.

"Can we?" she gasped, still enthralled with her newfound senses.

"Of course, I think you'll like it."

I opened the sturdy oak door and and led us inside, the quaint shop furnished with just a few simple wooden tables and chairs scattered near the cozy entranceway. Breads and jams of every flavor imaginable lined the walls, adding a visual accompaniment to the bouquet of smells that greeted each visitor.

Peering over the assortment laid out in front of us, I decided on a loaf of cinnamon-honey bread, the bakery's most popular item – when I asked the girl what she wanted, she said to leave it a surprise, so I figured this was a reasonably safe bet. After handing the cashier a few bills, I brought our small bounty to one of the tables (which were really just barrels with wooden boards nailed on top, though this only added to the rustic atmosphere) by the window. Since she was still taking everything in, the girl had immediately chosen a seat where she could watch what was going on outside.

As we began to dig in to our simple meal, the girl's face lit up once again with a euphoria not far off from that of some miraculous awakening.

"I take it they don't have anything like this where you're from?"

"NO. Thish ish delishosh! Ife nefer tasted hufan food befoh, but thish is amathing." She was so taken with her food that she hadn't bothered to swallow before responding, forcing me to hold back my own giggling.

"Whath tho funny?" she asked, pouting.

"Nothing, nothing – you can be kind of adorable, is all." The girl's cheeks reddened as she dropped her gaze, though I was able to catch the slightest hint of a smile creep onto her lips. "Speaking of which, I don't think I ever asked you what your own world is like."

We were tucked away in a secluded enough spot that, coupled with the ever-present hum of ovens and chatter in the background, I was pretty sure we wouldn't be caught by any overly-curious eavesdroppers.

"Oh, you're right!" The girl bounced back up at my question, taking a reprieve from her food so she could more easily talk. "So humans all live in what we call the mortal realm, right?"

"I figured as much."

"And spirits come from a whooole bunch of different worlds, usually serving one specific purpose. Like, since I'm an aspect of death, I come from the realm of the dead –"

She paused for a moment and laughed nervously.

"But I guess you already knew that, huh?"

I gave a weak smile in response and allowed her to continue. "Most of the realm I come from, which we usually just call the Middle Place, is made up of a big, big forest, stretching out in every direction. That's why we're needed to help souls move on – without someone to help them, they tend to wander and get lost, or never even leave the foyer in the first place."

"The foyer?"

The girl nodded as she looked down at her plate, pushing a scrap of bread around with her finger. "Mhm, until a mortal's soul is ready to move on, they stay in this sort of mansion. That's the foyer. Each soul is given their own room to prepare for their final journey, although – "

She stared out the window with a sad smile as an endless crowd of people walked by, each in their own separate worlds.

"Compared to a place like this, it was pretty drab and lonely."

"So then where did you live, er– reside?"

Maybe a poor choice of words there.

"Oh, in the same place!"

The girl either didn't notice, or simply didn't mind, my potential faux pas.

"All the spirits in my world do. Besides guiding souls there and out, we sometimes help them let go of their lives in the mortal realm. That's, um, actually how we met…" She tapped two fingers together and glanced up at me.

"I – "

Thinking, thinking, thinking, and – nope, still nothing.

"I don't remember," I said, dejected.

The girl began to swing her legs under the table as she continued playing around with the crumbs in front of her. "I don't think anyone can blame you for that. Like I said before, mortals don't typically cross from one world to another, so they have a hard time holding on to their memories."

"Then…could you tell me more about what it was like? When we first met, I mean." I offered what I hoped was a reassuring smile. "Even if I can't remember right now, that doesn't mean it's not important to me."

"I-If you really want…" the girl murmured, a faint blush rising in her cheeks once more. "When I had taken you to the room you'd be staying in, you actually asked me to stay and talk to you. You couldn't remember a lot about who you were or where you came from, but none of that seemed to matter. We talked for hours and hours, and every time I came to visit you, you had more to say."

She giggled and shook her head, reflecting on some fond memory we didn't share. "It was a little confusing at first, trying to understand why a mortal would want me around so much. And for a while, I thought I was just helping you move on and let go of your past life, but then – "

She placed her hands over her chest and closed her eye.

"That warm feeling started up inside. And the more I was around you, the more it grew and grew. When you told me that it sounded like love, and told me what that meant, I knew I wanted to ask you to…to be my boyfriend. You don't think that's crazy, do you?" She said this last part in a whisper, like she was sharing some deep secret.

"No, no, of course not!" Her story was certainly fantastical, but it wasn't much weirder than anything else she had already told me. "Even if I don't remember all the details, I still feel like the luckiest guy in the world to be able to go on a date with a girl as cute as you."

Flustered by this unexpected compliment, the girl started to play with the bangs covering her right eye, mumbling, "I-I'm really not that cute…"

It was then that I really began to notice how careful she was to never move that little bit of hair away. I thought for a moment about asking her why that was, but swiftly decided against it – even if we were "dating", we had only just started to get to know one another. Whether it was simply a stylistic choice, or there was something she was trying to hide, I was certain she'd tell me all about it when she was ready.

"So…" I said slowly, trying to pick up the conversation again, "is there anything you want to know about me? Now that I have most of my memory back, at least."

I popped a piece of bread in my mouth as I waited for her response.

"Do you love me?"

"Do I love…"

As understanding dawned on me, I took a deep breath, lodging that little bit of food in my throat and forcing me to reel back, coughing and sputtering – it was clear that this girl didn't mind moving fast, but how was I supposed to answer a question like that on the first date?!

"I, uh, that's – "

How was I supposed to answer truthfully without either hurting her feelings or trampling all over the potential for a real relationship to blossom?

"You see, love…love is something very special, and it takes time to develop between two people, and – it, uh, might take a little longer to grow between us, too."

"Ohh…" The girl nodded along, taking it all in. It didn't seem like she was hurt or offended – she really did just want to know if I loved her. "So love needs time – what else?"

"Um, I guess - " I wasn't sure how exactly I could teach someone else about love when I didn't even have any experience myself. "You need to care about each other, and should try to do things the other person likes. Y'know, make them feel special, make them feel happy."

The girl listened with rapt attention, hanging on each and every word.

"And most of all, it's a feeling from deep inside, I think. So when you know, you'll know."

I knew it was a half-baked answer, and I felt guilty that the best I could offer were some vague clichés that didn't actually explain much, but the girl seemed more than satisfied with what sparse knowledge I could pass on to her, and returned to what remained of her meal with renewed gusto.

4

After finishing up the last of our (admittedly meager) breakfast, I left the bakery hand-in-hand with the stranger I now called my girlfriend. We took our time meandering over to the next destination (a nice change of pace from that morning's excitement), chatting about all the little things the city had to offer. I felt a bit like a tour guide on their first day, as I floundered about trying to come up with an adequate explanation for each new sight and sound and smell the girl came across. Still, her endless sense of wonderment made up for whatever deficiencies I had in my role as host, and she seemed hardly disappointed with my efforts.

A few minutes of sunny strolling later, and we arrived at a mid-tier shop that catered to a fairly wide range of tastes (and budgets). I never had much interest in fashion myself, so my experience in clothes shopping, especially when it came to that of the fairer sex, was…limited, to put it kindly. Given this, and being unable to think up any better strategy, I suggested we start at the front of the store and work our way to the back – it'd be a slow process, but I was sure we'd find at least a couple of things she liked that way.

This was somewhat hampered by the fact that, despite my continued attempts to tease out what kind of style she liked, the girl would only shake her head and wander off, saying "Whatever you think would look good on me." Needless to say, this was easier said than done.

As I sifted through endless racks of colorful garments, I struggled to find a single piece of clothing that felt like it'd fit her. This one was too frilly, that one too plain, another wasn't the right size – sure, there was no doubt she'd look *good* in any of these, but since she was relying on my discretion, I wanted to find something that wasn't simply "nice". I wanted to get her something that had a little more thought and care put into it, and so –

"Yuu?" A curious voice reached out to me. "What are you doing here?"

Himeo ran over with a few shirts hung over her arm, visibly confused.

"Oh, ya know, just…shopping." I quickly threw the skirt I was holding back onto the clothes pile behind me.

"…In the women's department?"

"Don't judge me."

Before she had a chance to respond, I felt my entire body go cold as my spirited friend rushed over and threw her arms around my waist.

"Boo," she whispered in my ear, squeezing my midsection.

"Well hello, who's this?" Himeo asked, eying the girl with a frightening smile.

My mind started racing – how the hell was I supposed to explain this to her? "Oh yeah, for some reason I died while walking home yesterday and came back to life and now I'm dating Death herself." I was hoping I'd have at least another day or two to come up with a convincing cover story, since, even if I bought into all this craziness, there was no reason to think anyone else would do the same.

"Uh, you see, this is – "

"I'm his girlfriend!" the head resting on my shoulder explained cheerfully.

There was only a brief pause, though I could have sworn the entire city went silent at that very moment.

"I…don't think Yuu ever mentioned you before – when did you both start dating?"

"Just yesterday – !"

"She moved here," I finished for her. "We had been talking online for a while, but she only had a chance to come here recently. She'll, uh – "

C'mon, think, think…

"She's staying with me until her apartment is set up, since I have an extra room and all. And that's why we're here now – she wasn't able to bring all her things with her, so we're grabbing some new clothes while we can."

Not the best lie, but there was enough truth sprinkled in that I hoped it'd be believable enough.

"I don't get why you're always like that. You never even mentioned that you were talking to a girl in the first place – " Himeo leaned forward for a closer inspection. "And such a cutie, too!"

The girl clasped her hands together and looked down at the ground, whispering, "I'm not that cute…"

Déjà vu, I suppose.

"Oh! And I completely forgot to introduce myself – my name's Himeo, I'm Yuu's friend from school."

The spirit took a step out and gave a small bow, returning the greeting.

"So, have you found anything you like yet?" Himeo asked as

the girl continued to stand half-hidden behind me.

She thought for a moment, then shook her head. "Not really. I don't know much about clothing in this world, so I'm not exactly sure what would look good on me."

Himeo gave a small laugh and shook her head, thankfully glossing over the strange wording. "I figured as much. Yuu won't mind if I take you away from him for a bit, right? We can get your measurements, and I know I'll do a better job of helping you find something you love."

"Would you mind?" I asked, glancing at the pile of clothes I had just finished rummaging through. "I'll admit I'm...kind of in over my head here."

"Yeah, yeah, what are friends for?" Himeo said as she started to lead the girl away. The spirit glanced back at me with some trepidation, but I motioned her to go on ahead.

"It's alright, like she said - she'll be way more help to you than me. I'll meet you back here when you're all done, ok?" The girl flashed an uncertain smile and nodded, running off to catch up with Himeo.

I whiled away the rest of my time looking through the rows of dresses hung a few sections over. I thought about picking out a gift myself, then quickly recalled why I had handed my girlfriend off to Himeo in the first place. Still, couldn't hurt to try, right?

* * *

About 30 minutes of fruitless searching and sizing and comparing had passed when both girls returned, several bundles wedged under each arm.

"She should be set for a while," Himeo said with a relieved

sigh. "I also took the liberty of getting her fit for a school uniform, since I assume she'll be going to the same school."

School! That had somehow completely slipped my mind – it wasn't like I could leave the girl alone by herself all day, so having her go to school with me would be the most direct way to get around that issue. Of course, that also brought with it a whole different set of problems.

"Y-yeah, thanks," I murmured, trying to think of how I could familiarize a stranger to this world with the concept of school over a single day.

As we waited in line to check out, Himeo gave me a light jab me with her elbow. I leaned down towards her as she whispered, "Don't worry about her enrolling – I'll pull some strings and make sure she's all set for Monday."

"You can do that?"

Himeo raised one eyebrow. "If not me, who else?"

"Point taken. You're a serious life-saver, though. If there's anything I can do to help you – "

"Oh don't worry," she said glancing towards the spirit, who was currently invested in inspecting each of the fake flowers flanking the store's entrance with careful scrutiny. "I know you will."

With this mysterious assurance, we finished paying for our purchases and started to go our separate ways. As me and the girl walked down the sidewalk leading out of the city, however, I heard Himeo shout, "Have fun tonight you two!" as she sprinted away, laughing to herself. I looked to the spirit to see if she had any idea as to what Himeo meant, but she had quickened her pace and already made it a fair distance away. With a helpless shrug I ran after her, soon forgetting about the whole incident.

Nearing the edge of the city limits, we passed by a small pond set against the path. The sun was starting to descend into the water, casting the banks in a deep crimson; coupled with the crisp brown and orange leaves scattered all around, it was about as ideal an autumn view as one could ask for.

"Y'know, it's funny," I said as I took a seat on one of the benches facing the pond. "If you took a picture of it, I don't think you could tell the difference between a sunset and a sunrise this time of year."

"Are they really so different in the first place?" the girl asked plainly.

"What do you mean?"

"If you couldn't tell the difference, would it make it any different to you?"

I turned to study her face, searching for a deeper meaning to her words, but, as so often seemed to be the case, she only bore an earnest smile as she continued to stare out at the calm waters.

"Maybe not, but - I'd still miss the morning if it never happened, y'know?"

"Mm."

The girl nodded her head, but said no more. Maybe she trusted me to understand what she meant, or maybe there really was no deeper meaning to her words. Either way, I was beginning to feel like the more straightforward she was with me, the less I actually understood her.

Regardless, it was nice to sit together a while longer in comfortable silence, admiring the peaceful scenery – things had been fairly hectic since morning, so it was a refreshing change of pace to be able to take a break and relax for a little. Just as I was about to suggest we start walking home again, the girl pointed to a bunch of white flowers floating by the muddy edges of the pond.

"What are those?"

"Oh, these?"

I got up and walked over to the wooden fence that served to keep wayward pedestrians from falling into the water – with an abundance of trees from the surrounding park, the nights were exceptionally dark in this area. I bent down and snuck my hand through a convenient opening in the boards, plucking one of the flowers out of the water. As I returned to the bench, I pulled off the roots and shook away the remaining droplets of water so I could place it behind the girl's ear.

"It's a water lily – it's kind of rare to see them in bloom around this time of year, but nature can be weird like that."

The girl reached up and touched the flower tenderly, as if too sudden a movement might shatter it.

"Lily…thank you."

She leaned over and kissed my cheek softly – her lips, as might be expected, felt like a biting wind, though I couldn't say I didn't enjoy the sensation.

"Aha, what was that for?"

"That's my name…Lily." She smiled contentedly and held out her hand. With my heart aglow, I happily took it in mine as we continued on our way home together.

As soon as we stepped in the door, exhaustion flooded over me and, after telling Lily I would take a short nap, trudged my way upstairs and collapsed in bed.

First date, first kiss, first time going out in public together…it was a day of many firsts. Even if everything didn't go *entirely* like I'd planned, I couldn't deny that I felt, well – happy. It wasn't like I believed in love at first sight or anything, but I had to wonder if something like fate was what brought us together in the first place? I mean, I couldn't imagine human-spirit romances were all that common, and I'd never imagine I'd die before having my first girlfriend (though I had a feeling Jun might argue otherwise).

I buried my face against the pillow and soon drifted off to sleep, the question of romantic entanglement hanging on my mind. I woke up just an hour or two later to Lily's faint voice coming through the door.

"Yuu? Can I come in?"

Trying to get my bearings and adjust to the darkened room, I sat up and shook my head. "Yeah, of course. Door's unlocked."

Lily stepped out from behind the door, clad in nothing more than her undergarments. The light purple color and lacy design certainly complemented her figure, and oh my god she really had nothing else on.

As my brain began to fully process what, exactly, I was looking at, I tried my best to calm down so I wouldn't make the girl feel embarrassed or hurt her feelings by accident. After all, this was her first full day in this world, I couldn't expect her to understand all the social norms that inherent to it right off the bat.

Presuming that was the case, anyway.

"Um, if you don't mind me asking," I said carefully, clearing my throat. "Why aren't you wearing any clothes?"

Lily brought her hands together and shifted back and forth. Looking at her now, I could better appreciate how attractive her body really was. The dress she had been wearing since we met was a fairly modest one, and must've been concealing her more…curvaceous features. Maybe some of it was due to never having seen a real-life girl in this state of undress before, but I would've sworn at the time (and I'll be honest – still do) that I had never seen anything more attractive in my life.

"Himeo said that if I put this on tonight it'd make you happy, and I couldn't think of a way to thank you for our first date, so I'm sorry if it doesn't look right on me, I've never worn something like this before, and, and – "

"No, no! You look…you look amazing." From what I could tell, she was less embarrassed about being in this outfit, than she was worried that I might not like it.

Lily rushed over and pressed her body against mine, squeezing tight. "So it worked?" she asked with unbridled joy.

"Yeah, I'm, uh…I'm very happy."

We were wandering into dangerous territory here.

"Although I just remembered! We never had anything to eat for dinner – are you hungry? Why don't I head downstairs and whip something up real quick?"

Lily sprung back and gave a cheerful nod, apparently still oblivious to her own body. "I'll keep you company!"

I wasn't sure my heart would last if I had to deal with this much longer.

"Alright, but why don't you throw on some extra clothes first, that way you don't catch a cold. I'll get started on the cooking, and you can come down when you're ready."

As I moved to get out of bed and leave with my willpower intact, Lily spoke up again, her voice filled with heart-rending disappointment. "But…I thought you said this made you happy. Do you not like it?"

I let out a quiet sigh – I had a feeling this was what Himeo was talking about earlier. For as kind as she could be, she had a pension for pushing people's buttons that could, at times, border on the sadistic.

"No, no, I love how you look, it's just…"

I had trouble thinking of a way to politely explain what was wrong with her choice of attire, due in no small part to the lack of blood now running to my brain.

"The problem is you look *too* good, and I, uh – I don't think I deserve that kind of reward."

It wasn't a total lie – I had no idea what she saw in me, and it didn't feel right looking at her in such an intimate when it was doubtful that she even fully understood what she was doing.

"Don't say that!" Lily leaned forward, pressing her softness against my chest once more. "I'm happy to do anything for you so long as it makes you happy~"

If I didn't know better, I might've thought she was having fun torturing me.

In the end, Lily spent the rest of the night in that state of relative undress, either totally oblivious or completely uncaring with regard to its more nefarious effects on me, and when at last we crawled into bed for the night, she insisted on sleeping as she was. By this point my good sense was at its breaking point, so all I could do in response was welcome her under the sheets. However, now that there was a lack of clothes blocking her skin from mine, that nofastw-familiar freezing sensation overtook my entire body as she cuddled up next to me.

It may not have been a cold shower, but as they say – function over form.

5

When Monday soon rolled around Himeo proved to be as good as her word, and we had no issues getting Lily into our classes. I was hesitant at first about throwing her into something like this with so little time to prepare, yet – as seemed to be her approach when facing anything new – Lily greeted the opportunity with nothing less than heartfelt of enthusiasm and excitement. Still, I figured it was best to try and give her a crash-course on how everything worked the night before, hoping to prime her on what exactly to expect the following day, though, given her lack of any prior experience or context, I had to doubt how useful this really was.

Either way (prepared or not), the big day had arrived all the same, and we were fortunate enough to be able to claim a pair seats next to each other near the back of the class. Although Lily was enrolling partway through the semester, Himeo called in a few favors so she could join our class specifically – so far as she was willing to say, her argument rested on the fact that I would have the best chance of helping Lily adjust to the school, which the administration couldn't offer much of an argument against. Even if she was only a student, Himeo could be surprisingly persuasive with the faculty when she needed to be (a skill that did not go unappreciated during her tenure on the student council).

Once the first bell rang, the din of early morning conversations began to die down, and all the students worked their way back to their respective seats. The homeroom teacher, a relatively young woman compared to the other staff, entered the classroom a few moments later and gave her standard, rushed good morning as she quickly shuffled through a pile of papers on her desk. After getting organized a few moments later, she started to read off the usual school announcements, but paused when she looked up and spotted Lily.

"Ah, I almost forgot! We have a new student joining us today." She waved her hand back and smiled pleasantly. "Why don't you come up and introduce yourself?"

Lily hopped up from her seat and headed to the front of the classroom, a flurry of murmurs following in her wake.

"Pretty cute, huh?"

"Yeah, she's got the whole goth thing going on."

"What's with her eyes though?"

"What about them?"

"They were like…grey or something. Never seen that before."

"I dunno, maybe contacts?"

While Lily didn't look too out of place from a distance, her distinct eye color and ashy skin were liable to make her stand out on closer inspection. Still, she didn't seem to hear (or at least be bothered by) these remarks and, upon reaching the front desk, turned around and gave an energetic wave in my direction, which I meekly returned.

"Why don't you tell the class your name and say a little bit about yourself?" the homeroom teacher suggested.

Lily gave a small bow and glanced around at all the other students. "Hi everyone, um, my name is Lily, and I've never actually gone to school before."

Oh boy.

"You mean, like in this area?"

Lily nodded and pointed to me as she continued to address the teacher. "I only came here a few days ago, so I'm staying with Yuu for now."

I could feel a thousand daggers being shot my way, but my classmates' misplaced jealousy was the least of my concerns. I focused all my attention forward and prayed she wouldn't say anything weirder than that, letting everyone forget about it and move on by next period.

"Well, that's, erm - very kind of him to help you," the teacher said, caught off-guard by Lily's frank admission. "Is there anything the class should know about you?"

"Oh, yes! I'm a spirit."

Ah. There it was.

"A...spirit?" the teacher repeated, after Lily bowed once more and made her way back to her desk.

I shot up from my seat before Lily had a chance to say anything more. "A, uh, spirit-*ed* student is what she meant."

Was anyone really going to buy that?

"Since it's her first day, she's still a little nervous, but she wanted everyone to know that she's really...really excited to be here." I sunk back down in my chair, having drawn an undue amount of attention to myself again. "That - that's all."

Thankfully, the teacher only gave an incredulous nod and returned to the announcements. Even if what I said wasn't entirely convincing, she had more important things to worry about than the weird things one of her students was babbling about.

Already feeling drained before the day had even started, I

pulled out a scrap of paper and scribbled a few words, passing it to Lily while the teacher was otherwise distracted.

Remember, people don't know spirits exist.

She glanced at what I had written and jotted down her own response.

Some.

Lily stuck her tongue out playfully and then turned her attention back to the front of the classroom. I sighed and followed suit, shaking my head – every day was sure to be an adventure with her around.

At least the rest of the morning went by without any further slip-ups. Lily seemed to enjoy learning anything she could about humans and our world, and, against all odds, I was able to immerse myself back into some sense of normality again, going from class to class and focusing on taking notes and getting through the day. Before I knew it, the lunch bell had rung and our usual trio – now with an additional member – pulled our desks together to eat.

"So who's this fine specimen you've brought for us today?" Jun asked as Lily took her place next to me.

"It's his girlfriend, so you can settle down already," Himeo said flatly. "Though…now that I think about it, I don't think you ever told me your name the other day."

I gave a silent thanks that we had somehow managed to dodge that particular bullet.

"It's Lily," she said with a warm smile, reflexively bringing her hand behind her ear where the flower had been.

"You already know Himeo," I explained, "and this is Jun, who you're best off avoiding entirely."

"Hey hey hey! Don't be like that." I pushed Jun's arm away as he leaned over to try and ruffle my hair. "I've been looking out for this guy since we were only this big." He held his hand a foot off the ground as Himeo rolled her eyes and Lily giggled along – it somehow felt like she'd always been a part of our group.

"So Lily," Jun continued, unfazed by his earlier mistake. "What led you to come all the way out here? Wanted to be closer to your lover?" He flashed a mischievous, though not ill-intended, grin in her direction.

"W-We're not lovers yet," Lily said quietly, blushing faintly. "Yuu promised to teach me everything he knows though, so…so until then I'll still be learning."

She looked up at Jun and Himeo, who bore expressions halfway between shock and hilarity.

"Er, it's good that you two can be so, ah…'open' about these kinds of things. I'm sure he'll treat you well." For once, Jun didn't seem keen to press the issue, perhaps realizing Lily was one enigma it'd take a little longer to unravel.

"More importantly, we're just happy you're here with us now," Himeo added.

Lily thanked her happily, and the two began to chat about classes, with Himeo asking how her day had been and how she liked this new school, and Lily offering up a hundred different questions I hadn't been able to answer myself. I was relieved to see that the two of them were becoming fast friends, as it was easy to see Himeo genuinely cared about Lily, treating her with a kindness that extended well beyond simple courtesy. Whether this stemmed from some sense of responsibility as student council president, or just derived from sisterly instinct, it was good to see that Lily would have at least one other person she could rely on both in and out of school.

As Himeo and Lily continued their own conversation, Jun

grabbed my shoulder and pulled me aside, speaking in a hushed voice. "Alright, don't take this the wrong way, but I have to ask – what's up with your girlfriend?"

"What do you mean?"

"C'mon, cut the crap. The way she looks, showing up one day out of nowhere, saying she's a spirit – is this some kind of weird roleplay thing? I mean don't get me wrong, I'm not judging if it is, but as your friend I want to know what's really going on."

I sighed and met Jun's stare directly – he may not believe me, but I couldn't deny that he was the closest friend I had. If I could confide in anyone, it would have to be him.

"Look – "

Before I could confess the truth, the sounds of an explosion rocketed through the hallway. A cacophony of screams and gasps soon followed as students scrambled to see what was going on, though by the time our group went to join the crowd of onlookers, the school had fallen silent once more.

"Maybe a pipe burst?" one person suggested. No one responded at fist, as everyone seemed to freeze with bated breath, awaiting the next explosion –

Though none came.

After a collective sigh of relief, a general chatter resumed as everyone in the classroom continued to speculate on what might've happened. A car crash outside? A window breaking? A meteor hitting the Earth? While some of the ideas posited were more plausible than others, it looked like no one was too terribly shaken up.

At least for a few seconds.

Without warning, the walls began to shake and the floor trembled. Even the windows could be heard rattling in their frames, as what sounded like heavy footsteps thundered outside.

Clearly having gotten their fill of excitement for the day, one student quickly slammed the classroom door shut, as the group that had gathered nearby immediately dispersed, leaving only the four of us standing in front of it. I tried to peer out the glass window, but all I could see was an empty hallway. Yet even so, I had a bad feeling about all this. Whatever was out there, I couldn't imagine it was anything good.

As I stepped back to join the rest of the class by the other side of the classroom, I recalled something Lily had said when she first showed up –

You can't die.

I hadn't given it much thought at first, but if what she said was true, then shouldn't I be doing something with it? I'd lived my whole life up until this point trying to avoid conflict, staying out of the way and keeping to myself – this could be my opportunity to change all that, and finally do something worth remembering.

I forced myself to turn back to Lily and asked her bluntly: "What you said the other day, about being together and – " I glanced toward Jun and Himeo, who seemed preoccupied with what was going on outside. "Y'know, not dying. Was that true?"

She nodded hesitantly. "Like I said, I've never done this before, so I don't know how exactly how it all works, but – "

"I want to check out what's going on. If – " I know I sounded ridiculous, but it was too late to back out now. "If something's out there that might put the whole school in danger, I need to go out there and stop it."

I know, I know. It was a line straight out of a cheesy action movie, but for once, I felt something *real*. Some compulsion to get out and act, instead of hanging back and staying quiet. A faint flicker of familiarity crossed my mind, though at the time what relation it had to the current situation I couldn't say.

Either way, the time to act was now. I took a deep breath and reached for the doorknob, as a sudden chill coursed through my body.

"I'm coming with you," Lily said firmly, her hand placed over mine.

This is the point in the story where the hero is supposed to tell his love interest to stay behind and keep safe, but really – who was I kidding? I would need all the help I could get, so I gave a single nod and slipped out the door with Lily undetected, completely ignorant as to what might be waiting nearby.

I quickly scanned the hallway, but, other than a disquieting silence, nothing seemed to be out of place. Lacking any clear direction or plan, we started walking towards one end of the hall, a grim tension rising as things remained unnervingly peaceful.

"What do you think happened?" Lily asked as we passed by another darkened classroom.

"I'm not sure, to be honest. It could be an earthquake or something, but…"

"But?"

"We don't really get those in this area."

Lily pressed herself against my arm, bearing a worried smile. "Maybe it really is nothing? If we haven't heard anything yet, then it's probably – "

Before she could finish that thought, the trembling started up again with even greater severity. I whipped around, and, well –

Prior to meeting Lily, I may not have actually believed what I witnessed rounding the corner. A creature with the head of a bull head and a shaggy body, matted dark brown fur covered in flecks of debris, stood towering at the other end of the hallway. Its massive shoulders and muscular build mustered an imposing image, one that seemed none too keen on talking things out.

Yes, as impossible as it might seem, there was no mistaking it – that was an honest-to-god, straight-from-Greek-mythology, flesh-and-blood, really-standing-there-in-front-of-me, minotaur. Given a little more time, I might have retained some doubts as to what I was seeing. but that didn't seem to be a luxury I would be readily afforded.

The creature let out an ear-splitting bellow as it stamped the ground, each crash of its hooves sending reverberations through the walls themselves. This feeling – of staring down a rampaging monster, some unbelievable creature, all for the sake of protecting a relative stranger…

Why did it feel so familiar?

I tried to move, to act, to get out of the way or fight back, but it was no use – my muscles had completely frozen up. Was it out of fear? Indecision? Disbelief? I guess it didn't matter if my body ultimately wouldn't respond.

I had dragged us into this mess, and now what?

I came in with no plan, no strategy, no idea what I was doing. I was just…some guy. Some guy who wanted to be more than he actually was. I had only just been introduced to a world outside the tiny one I'd made for myself, and I was already screwing it up. Was there even any point –

"Yuu?"

Lily's voice snapped me out of these self-deriding thoughts.

"What should we do?"

Lily...that's right!

I wasn't alone, not anymore. I had someone to help me out, someone who was relying on me as much as I was on her. It wasn't a question of what I did to get us into this situation – it was how I'd get us *out* of it. And if my legs wouldn't let me run, then all I could do was stand and fight.

Having lost whatever minuscule patience it had to begin with, the minotaur charged forward, moving with remarkable agility given its size. I repositioned myself so that I was closer to its center, crouching down in the vain hope that I might be able to catch the monster as it ran into me.

"Alright Lily," I murmured. "Let's grab the bull by the ho–"

This pithy quip was (for better or worse) cut short by a sudden pain in my abdomen, as I was swiftly lifted up into the air and carried away. It didn't take long to realize that, in an effort to stamp out my overwhelming fear, I sort of overdid it and...got impaled by the minotaur's horns.

As I undulated against the creature's head while it continued its relentless charge down the hallway, I had time to reflect on the mess I'd gotten myself into.

Is bravery that can't be backed up by ability just recklessness? Was I really trying to fight to protect everyone, or was I simply acting out of a burgeoning sense of inadequacy that had only recently come to light in view of my inevitable graduation and entry into the "real world"? After all, even if you were to bestow extraordinary power on someone like me, that hardly changes the person they are at their core. Even if one could escape death, what value did it retain if they could not make use of it?

I might've continued to opine on the nature of my existence

had the minotaur not reached the end of the hall, and – having finally taken notice of his incidental passenger – thrashed around wildly, sending my body this way and that. At this point the nausea from being swung around was going to surpass any pain from having a horn thrust through my stomach.

At least Lily was right about one thing – it looked like I really couldn't die. Of course, that wasn't much help in getting me out of the rather precarious position I'd found myself in, but hey, I was still alive – that had to count for something, right?

As I tried to pry myself free, I spotted Lily unfurling her white ribbon, which she whipped straight into a scythe once more. As she calmly approaching the beast, I noticed that something seemed…different. At first I thought it must've been due to the sheer intensity she was now emanating, each stride forward as delicate as it was deliberate, but it was clear something more was going on as soon as she spoke up.

"Let go of him."

Gone was the shy timidity or gentle playfulness that so often punctuated her words – it was like an entirely different person had taken over, driven by a single-minded determination and overwhelming confidence. The monster itself seemed almost baffled as well, tilting its head to the side as Lily stood directly in its path. However, this brief reprieve went as quickly as it came, and, after rearing its head low, readied to charge again.

Lily, for her part, didn't flinch in the slightest. She held her ground and casually leaned against her scythe, as if there wasn't even a threat to begin with. When the creature finally rushed forward, she smoothly turned to the side and pointed her blade at the creature.

"I said. LET. GO."

I could only glimpse what happened next, but the glint of

metal passing by seemed to indicate that Lily had managed to get her scythe around the creature's abdomen. With one quick jerk, she brought the monster (and, by extension, me) tumbling to the ground. She peered down at the creature, her eye devoid of any passion or emotion.

"You don't belong here. Begone."

With one fell motion, she ran her scythe across the monster's front, spraying a thin splatter of red across her face. The monster lurched forward as its body crumbled apart into nothingness, leaving behind a small, blue flame, which soon faded away as well.

Still trying to process this sudden turn of events, it only occurred to me that I was sprawled out on the ground when Lily walked over and bent down, offering me her hand. I shakily accepted it and returned to my feet, a knot forming in my stomach as I noticed, underneath the blood splatter coating her cheeks, Lily's features had softened once more, her expression no longer blank or expressionless. Before I could ask about what just happened, however, I felt a fresh chill as she threw her arms around me.

"A-are you ok? I never should have let that happen to you I'm so sorry how are you can you walk are you in pain you're still ok right – ?"

Lily fired off a rapid string of questions as she looked at me with a care and kindness so at odds with the presence I saw a few moments ago. Since we had only been "dating" for a couple days, it was possible that that was some other side to her personality I hadn't even considered. Or…was that just who she really was? Could it be that her cheery, if often shy, veneer was nothing more than that – a cover?

"I'm…I'm fine, really." I awkwardly smudged the bright red

dots off her face and forced a smile. While I couldn't deny that she just saved my life (again), a shadow of fear had marred my appreciation.

"I told you, even if you can't die, you can still be injured…" Lily ran her hand along my stomach, causing me to wince. "Ah, I'm sorry! I just – I wanted to see how deep it was. Does it hurt?"

Right now she didn't seem that much different from any other time we'd been together. So where did that sudden change in personality come from? She usually was so friendly and carefree, and yet she killed that monster without a second thought. I mean – maybe it had to be done, but how was she able to do so with no hesitation?

"I think my uniform suffered more than I did, honestly," I said with a half-hearted laugh. It certainly didn't feel pleasant to be gashed like that, but the pain was nowhere near what I expected it to be. Besides, seeing that Lily was back to her "normal" self (assuming what I was seeing now was, in fact, normal for her) put my mind somewhat at ease.

"You…you promise you won't do anything like that again?" Lily asked softly.

"Yeah, I - " I rested my head against hers. "That was really dumb of me. I'm sorry for dragging you into something like that."

"No! No…no." Lily placed her hand against my chest, balling up a part of my shirt. "I'd do anything for you. I'll…I'll always take care of you."

There was a lot I didn't know about her – no one could deny that. But if I needed to remember anything, it was that Lily…was Lily. That was enough for now.

"Thanks Lily. But still – " I pulled out my shirt, the lower half stained a dark crimson, and grimaced. "Probably wouldn't be a bad idea to get this patched up sooner rather than later. Can you walk with me to the nurse's office?"

Lily nodded and gently wrapped her arm around my side, allowing me to lean on her as I limped down the hallway. As we turned the corner and passed by a set of windows lining the wall, I spotted a number of white trucks and vans parked in front of the school's gate. I would've expected the police to show up first, but they looked more like the sort of vehicles used by the city's groundskeepers, and lacked any obvious signifiers that might suggest they belonged to any kind of first responders. While I knew this was more than a little strange ordinary, at the time I felt more relieved than anything – if the cops did show up, I had no idea how I'd be able to explain what happened (or where this big hole in my stomach came from).

I decided to put all those potential worries aside for the time being; there was enough on my mind as it was. Where did the monster come from? Was it somehow related to Lily showing up here? And what triggered that change in personality? Even if I was willing to accept that as a part of her, I still wanted to understand what it was, and where it came from.

I thought about asking her all about it right then and there, but Lily had been pretty reticent since we started walking, and I got the feeling that now wasn't the best time to get into something quite so heavy. Instead, we went on side by side in silence, each of our innermost thoughts and fears hidden from the other.

After treading down a few flights of echoing stairwells and further empty hallways, we at last reached our destination. As soon as I stepped into his office, the nurse - a tall man with short, dark hair and wide, round-frame glasses - glanced over the gouge on my abdomen and set about cleaning and disinfecting it. He was a somewhat strange fixture of the school, known around the student body for his supposed discretion, simply treating whatever injuries or ailments were presented to him with few questions asked. Even though no one seemed to know much more about him than that, he was fairly well-liked for these same discrete tendencies.

The nurse mumbled a few unintelligible words that seemed more directed at himself than either me or Lily, and motioned for me to take off my shirt. I gingerly unbuttoned the front and set it to the side, allowing him to swiftly stitch up the gash – despite my worst fears, it looked like the injury wasn't as bad as it could've been. Still, the needle stung all the same as it swerved in and out of my skin, so I looked for Lily to try to start up a fresh conversation and take my mind off the discomfort. I spotted her hiding in the corner, cheeks flushed and looking down.

"Hey, er – Lily, you ok?"

She jumped when I called out to her, jerking her head up for just a moment before turning back around to face the wall.

"Yes I'm fine all ok here!" She dropped her voice as she kicked one foot against the ground. "Just…tell me when it's over, please."

I hung my head and looked straight again – since Lily didn't seem to be in a very talkative mood, the best I could do was try to lose myself in thought until it was all over.

Trying my best to ignore the consistent sting of the needle, I went over everything I already knew. It had to be more than a coincidence that in the same week I find out spirits are real, a monster shows up out of nowhere. Lily hadn't mentioned anything about monsters or mythological creatures, but I still felt it was possible, if not likely, that this was linked to her in some way, though the specifics of this relationship would elude me for some time.

At least, given the absence of ambulances outside and any other students in the nurse's office, it seemed safe to assume that no one else had been seriously injured, which was an unexpected piece of good news. Though that still left the question as to *how* something like that showed up in the school with no one noticing. And why here of all places? Was it somehow attracted to Lily, since she was a spirit? It might make sense that two things not from this world would gravitate towards one another, but - the more I tried to piece together this mystery, the more questions presented themselves.

I let out a resigned sigh – I'd have to try to hide this incident from my friends, too. I felt bad for lying to them, but if I didn't think they'd believe me about Lily, they'd think I'd completely lost it if I tried to tell them I saw a real-life monster on top of that.

With one final pull of the needle, and a deft knot tied at the end, the nurse murmured something akin to "All done" and threw a few pieces of gauze onto my lap. I tried to thank him for his help, but as soon as I had put my shirt back on and gathered up my belongings, he had scooted back to his desk, totally invested in whatever he was now scribbling down, as if oblivious to my and Lily's presence.

Figuring we didn't have any more business here, I took Lily's hand and started heading back to class – I could only hope that no one noticed how long we were gone for, or wondered where we had disappeared to. For a while neither of us said a word, though I decided to finally break the silence once we approached the classroom door.

"Lily, y'know, I – "

For as much as I had wanted to say a few minutes ago, it felt like nothing sensible would come forth now. And yet, I still felt the need to say *something* – anything.

"I'm sorry I caused you so much trouble. I guess…I guess I'm still figuring out what to do with your gift, if that makes sense. I thought having that kind of power meant I should try my best to use it to help others, but I think I only ended up making things worse."

Lily squeezed my hand and turned towards me, her voice full of pity.

"No…no, I'm the one who should be sorry. I shouldn't have let you go out there like that in the first place and get hurt. You're only a human, and yet – well, no one's ever tried to protect me like you did. Watching you stand up for me, it – it made me happy." She dropped her gaze for a moment, looking back up at me with a pained expression. "Why is that?"

Even if in my heart I knew the answer, I couldn't answer her truthfully. Not yet.

"I…can't say for sure, but I think everyone wants to feel like they're cared for by someone. Like they have someone looking out for them."

A faint tint rose in Lily's pale cheeks.

"Does…that mean you care about me?"

"I, uh – " Her direct nature still caught managed to catch me off guard more often than not. "Y-yeah, of course I do. Although I don't think I've done a good job of it so far."

We shared a small laugh as Lily wrapped her arms around me, the chill I'd come to expect absent from her embrace.

"Please remember what I said, ok?" She squeezed me gently before pulling away. "You don't need to put yourself in harm's way to show me you care. I only want you to be you."

"Deal. Now let's – "

Bing bong~

The school's announcement bell rang over the intercom system as a staticky voice blared through the hall.

"We would now like to formally dismiss all remaining teachers and staff. Please check your email in the following days for updates."

With a loud "click", the announcement was over and the school was quiet once more.

"I guess they already let all the students go home once everything looked safe," I offered. "Why don't we grab our bags and do the same?"

After packing away a couple notebooks and discarding our half-eaten lunches, we set out for the school gates. Along the way, I spotted other parts of the building where the minotaur must have passed through – tiles torn up, large parts of the walls chipped away, doors torn off their hinges. I still had a hard time believing the same girl that was clinging to me now, as if terrified that another monster might show up at any moment, was able to defeat something like that so effortlessly. Maybe because she was a spirit of death, she was used to taking lives?

That…had its own unsettling implications.

A minute later and we made it outside, though before we could take even take one step further, we were accosted by a thin man in sunglasses. He looked like to be in his early 30s, and although he had on a crisp, black suit, the wrinkled dress shirt he wore underneath belied a bit of the rigid formality his ensemble tried to project. I had hoped to keep walking and pass him by without a second thought, but the fact that he was standing right in front of us, barring the way, more or less eliminated that option.

"You two – would you mind if I had a word with you?"

Despite the man's attempt at sounding authoritative, the exhaustion in his voice was plain to hear. Whether this was necessarily due to overwork or boredom, however, was difficult to say.

"Yeah, sure." I tightened my grip around Lily's hand. "Is something the matter?"

The man exhaled slowly and straightened his tie, trying to hide what I assumed was his own discomfort with the situation. "My name is Richard Braddock, though you can call me Rick. I work for a city agency that specializes in dealing with 'unusual' accidents. I just have a few basic questions I wanted to ask you, and then I'll let you be on your way." He introduced himself with the kind of tired disinterest that suggested he'd done this a thousand times before.

"A-alright."

"First off – do either of you attend this school?"

I glanced at Lily, who was eyeing the man carefully. I was starting to think I should fear more for his safety than our own.

"Yes, we – both of us do."

"Good, good. There were reports of an explosion inside your school not too long ago." I couldn't see his eyes through the jet black sunglasses he had on, but I felt them narrow in on me all the same. "You wouldn't happen to know anything about that, would you?"

"N-no, not really. We heard a loud bang about half an hour ago, but that was it."

Our impromptu interrogator took out a bent pad of paper

from his jacket pocket and began to jot something down. "And where were you at the time?"

"We were inside our classroom. With the rest of the students," Lily said flatly.

"Is that so?" Rick stopped writing and looked up at her. "Then you should know that all the students were evacuated some time ago."

Feeling my heart pound against my chest, I tried to steady my voice. "We – we didn't hear anything about that."

"Alright…" Rick sighed and rubbed the bridge of his nose, dispelling some of the tension that had been building up between us. "I'm gonna level with you kids. I don't think either of you were trying to get into any trouble, so just tell me straight – why are you only leaving the school now?"

While I tried to think of a response, some plausible excuse we could use to get out of this awkward confrontation, Lily spoke up again.

"We heard a loud noise and wanted to see what was happening, so we left the classroom to look around." She paused, her voice lowering. "Is that a problem?"

I wanted to stop her before things escalated any further, but my mouth was dry and no words would sputter forth. All I could do was trust that she knew what she was doing, and that her "other" side wouldn't come out again.

"Not necessarily." Rick paused, checked around to see if anyone else was nearby, and leaned close. "For sake of my own curiosity, what'd you find?"

"I'm…not sure you would believe me if I did tell you," I said slowly.

He let out a harsh, muted laugh. "I've seen a lot of things, I've heard a lot of things, and I've done a lot of things – I don't think you can surprise me."

I glanced at Lily, unsure as to what to do next. Rick seemed sincere enough, and I already let slip just now that we *had*, in fact, seen something in the school. Maybe it would be easier to come right out and tell him everything.

"There was…some kind of monster in there." I pointed back at the school, where a number of shattered windows flecked the otherwise near-impressively bland façade.

"A monster, you say?"

"A minotaur," Lily clarified. "Y'know, that thingy with horns?" She held two fingers up on either side of her head to illustrate.

"We found it running around the halls, and wanted to stop it before anyone got hurt."

Rather than look at us with incredulity, the man chuckled and shook his head as he stood back up, muttering "Not again," under his breath.

"You…believe us?" I asked.

"You kids don't look like you're all that shaken up after seeing something like that. Would I be wrong to suggest you know about the worlds that exist outside this happy little rock we're living on?"

"Wait, you know about those too?"

Rick nodded, glancing back at the numerous vehicles positioned behind him. "Not as much as I'd like, but enough to know they're as real as your or me."

"Th-then yeah, I know a little bit, too."

"I'm from the afterlife," Lily said plainly. "What he knows, he learned through me."

"A spirit, huh?" Lily nodded. "And you both took down that creature or whatever that was in there?"

"I mean, it was really more her than me," I mumbled.

"This is gonna be more of a headache than I'd hoped..." Rick took off his sunglasses, dark circles ringed beneath his eyes. "Come over here and I'll properly introduce myself."

Me and Lily followed him down the front steps and took a seat on the uneven stone as he tried to explain what exactly was going on.

"Like I said, my name is Rick. I work for a local government agency that deals with these kinds of, ah..." He waved his hand in the air, searching for the right word. "Let's say 'otherworldly' creatures. As you've probably already figured out, most people don't even know they exist, and it's my job to keep it that way."

I raised my hand. "Uh, question then."

"Go ahead."

"What does that have to do with us?"

"I'm getting there, I'm getting there." Despite looking only a few years older than us, I could hear him mutter something along the lines of "Kids these days, no patience" before continuing. "Standard protocol is to evacuate the area when an otherworldly being shows up, and quarantine the threat best we can. If possible, we like to do so with a certain amount of...discretion."

Rick squatted down and peered deeply at Lily. I didn't like the way he looked at her.

"This is the first time we've been beaten to the punch, however."

"So what is it you want from us then?"

I stole a glance in Lily's direction - she hadn't taken her eyes off of Rick this entire conversation.

"We don't know a whole lot about these monsters and spirits and whatever that come from these other realms. But we have learned one thing – they can't be hurt through any conventional means. So far as we've been able to find, only something from those other worlds can actually hurt them."

Like it or not, I was starting to see where he was going with this.

"Spirit or no spirit, I wanna know how you managed to kill what was in there."

"There's – I mean, we don't have to –" I tried to say something - anything - so Lily wouldn't have to, but she easily cut me off all the same.

"Did you know that escorting a mortal soul's and taking a creature's soul aren't all that different?" she said softly. "Or should I demonstrate right he– "

I squeezed her hand, trying to bring her back to reality.

"Yuu? I – " She looked at me as if in a daze. "I…I'm sorry. What I meant to say was that I was only trying to protect my boyfriend. I did what I had to, and that's it."

Thankfully Rick appeared to be unfazed by Lily's thinly-veiled threat, speaking with the same even tone as before. "Alright, looks like that's all I'll get out of you for today." He gave what I think was an attempt at a smile as he continued. "I don't really care if you're actually spirit or whatever, as long as you don't go around causing any trouble – deal?"

Lily nodded slowly. Her grim persona had already vanished once more, though she seemed to remain as doubtful as I was about Rick's true intentions.

"We'll cover up the damage here and get some kind of story out to the public so that no one panics. And needless to say – " He dropped his voice to just above a whisper. "Not a word of this gets out to anyone else. For your sake as much as mine."

Lily and I gave our silent assent.

"Good. And if you happen to run into any more creatures like that, make sure to reach out to me first."

Rick handed me a plain-looking business card with his name and phone number on it. The letters "PCU" were written on the top right corner, next to a multilayered triangle that must've served as the organization's logo.

"Look, I don't mean to be harsh with you kids. It's just - we've been getting more and more cases of these monsters and spirits showing up every day, and it's all we can do to keep things under wraps. And besides –" He ran a hand through his hair, as if still thinking about something else. "In a way, I understand what you're both going through. So, uh – take care on your way home."

And with that, Rick walked away, climbing into one of the blank vehicles and driving off with the rest of the fleet, leaving Lily and I to share a quiet walk home, wondering what this all meant for our not-so-simple life together.

6

Following our run-in with the minotaur, the school had to be closed for a few days to repair all the damage done. The official explanation being circulated was that a bull had somehow gotten loose from a truck and ran amok for a while before being safely captured by animal control. To be fair to Rick or whoever that concocted this story, it wasn't *too* far from the truth.

At least, with the extra free time we suddenly found ourselves with, I had the perfect opportunity to take Lily out and see some more of the local venues. She had already adapted surprisingly well to her new home life, but there was still a long way to go when it came to acting "normal" (for example, not telling everyone we came into contact with that she was a spirit), so giving her more exposure to the outside world seemed like a good way to work on that. And besides, we were technically dating – it only made sense that we'd actually go on a real date from time to time.

Lily, for her part, didn't have any place in particular that she wanted to go during our time off, so I figured – cliché as it may be – a walk in the park might fit the bill. Although the area was pretty lively, especially for a weekday afternoon (most likely due to a combination of the school being closed and the waning, mild fall weather), we were able to claim an unoccupied spot by the lake and laid out a small blanket to rest on. On our way over I had been asking Lily about what she thought about the human world so far, leading me to a concern I hadn't given much thought up until now.

"I know it's only been a few days, but do you miss your home?"

Lily remained quiet for a while as she leaned against my shoulder, looking over the water. "I've never really had a home. Not like this, at least." She turned to me as a glint of bittersweet melancholy passed her eye. "And I want to make this place my home. With you."

For some reason my heart skipped a beat hearing her say this. "W-well, yeah, I hope you're happy being here. But there must've been some kind of place that you lived, right? Like a - like a house or something?"

Lily shook her head slowly. "Each realm is different, but for spirits in the afterlife –"

She ran her hand through the grass, struggling to find the right words to express herself. Given that we (literally) came from two different worlds, I couldn't blame her.

"We don't live, not like mortals do. It's more like…like we just exist."

"I think I understand. And at the same time – "

A couple walked by with a stroller. An older man, leaning on a cane, hobbled past, smiling to himself. A couple of ducks that had been floating on the outskirts of the water sent ripples through the water as they took flight. The general hum of senseless conversations filled the air behind us.

"I guess I don't, or – maybe it's more like I can't."

Lily gave me a curious look and brought her face close to

74

mine. She seemed to have a habit of doing that whenever she was intrigued by what someone was saying. "What do you mean?"

"It's like…I've always assumed those two are the same thing. If you exist, you're alive. And if you're alive, you exist. But in a lot of ways, I think I'm starting to see that's not necessarily true, even if I still don't fully understand it myself."

Lily closed her eye and nodded, turning back towards the lake. "It's hard to compare the existence of humans and spirits, but I still like to think that there are others out just like me."

"What do you mean?"

"I want to think there are others who are happy, for one." She smiled faintly as she said this, looking out to a world I still could not see. "And who've found their own purpose."

"But didn't you say every spirit has their own responsibilities or functions, right?" I gave a pained smile as I tucked my knees closer to my chest. "I mean, it must be nice knowing you were made for a reason."

"Maybe…" She plucked a blade of grass and spun it between her fingers. "But what if that was all you ever knew?"

"Hm?"

"If there was an entire world out there that you never knew about, would you miss it?"

"I – I guess not, if I didn't even know it existed."

"That's what it's like being a spirit in my realm. The things I've felt and seen, the things I've experienced and done, I…I never could have understood them before coming here. But now that I am – " Lily nodded to herself, as if to reaffirm what she was about to say. "I know this is where I belong."

I stretched out on the blanket, the warmth of the sun and the chill of the autumn wind passing over my body. "Honestly,

I'm kind of relieved to hear that. I can't imagine what it's like to come to a completely different world, but as long as I know you're happy here, I won't have many wo–"

I suddenly felt Lily's hands on the back of my head as she slowly placed it on something soft. I opened my eyes to see her face beaming down at me.

"I doubt the ground is a very nice place to rest," she said tenderly.

"Oh, yeah, you're right," I murmured, trying to hide my obvious embarrassment. Lily's lap *did* make for an outstandingly comfortable pillow, though, and as I felt her fingers comb through my hair in gentle strokes, I couldn't help but start to doze under the afternoon sky.

* * *

I groggily awoke on the blanket a few minutes later, as Lily must've wandered off to some other part of the park while I was out.

"So much for not sleeping on the ground," I grumbled as I pushed myself up and tried to massage some of the soreness out of my neck.

I took a quick look around the park and spotted Lily over by the open field, kneeling down next to a rabbit and petting it with a look of sweet contentment. Normally any of the wild animals around here would've run off the second someone approached them, but this one seemed perfectly at ease in her presence. I had always heard that animals had senses beyond that of humans, so maybe it could somehow tell she was different? Either way, Lily seemed to be enjoying the company of her new friend, and so I decided to keep watching from afar rather than disturb them.

While she continued to play with the rabbit – it bounding after her hand every time she moved it away – I started to reflect on the nature of our own relationship. Or was it even a real relationship to begin with? If what Lily had told me was true, the reason we even started dating in the first place was mostly out of convenience – she wanted me to teacher her about love and see what the mortal world was like, and I didn't want to be, well, dead. If that's all there was to it, would it still be possible to build something more out of it?

Lily giggled to herself as the rabbit jumped onto her lap, sniffing her all over as if still trying to figure out what she really was. I smiled and shook my head.

Being around Lily, I felt happy.

More than that, actually.

It was a kind of easy comfort, the sort of thing you feel when you're around someone who lets you fully be yourself. Even if I had a million more questions about where she came from, who she was, and - hell - what she saw in me to begin with, I was certain that my burgeoning feelings for her went beyond simple gratitude. Maybe it wasn't yet love, but it had to be something more than friendship or novelty. Lily's innocent curiosity and earnest resolve had drawn me in, and I was fascinated with how different she viewed the world I'd taken for granted my entire life. Plus, I'd be lying if I said I didn't already see how much she cared about me.

So maybe it would take a little longer to figure out where these feelings would take me. For now, I was more than happy to share my otherwise-mundane life with this strange girl I'd found myself stuck with. Whatever the reason we came together, whoever she really was deep down inside, she was my girlfriend now. I would treat her like it.

Seeing as Lily was still preoccupied with her new friend, I decided to take a stroll around the path that circled the park. The air was crisp, with a slight sting in the lungs after a particularly cold gust blew past - a subtle reminder of winter's inevitable ascension. After a few minutes of walking, I reached the point where the park itself intermingled with the vanguard of buildings that served as an entrance to the city proper. Although this area was less crowded with architecture than the shopping district or residential area, the clash of towering structures against sprawling flatlands always looked a little jarring.

Continuing to wander past one of the many alleyways that fed into the main avenue, I picked up on a pair of hushed voices coming from nearby. Any other day I would've ignored it and kept walking (a pattern I would not pick up on until some time later), but, be it fate or a lack of self-preservation instincts, my curiosity got the best of me, and I decided to see what was going on.

Entering the alley, I could see two men huddled together with their backs to me, each wearing a heavy coat. The one on the left, who was also sporting a black winter cap, seemed to be speaking, but his voice was so low that I couldn't make out much of what he was saying. The man on the right was a bit shorter, though, considering I was looking at them from behind, the only other distinguishing trait I could make out was a mess of brown hair that went down to his shoulders. I was about to keep walking, leaving them to their own business, when I heard another voice rise above their murmuring, this time belonging to a woman.

"You have no right to demand that which does not belong to

you. I ask that you leave now so no harm may befall you."

Whoever this third person was, she certainly had a...*unique* way of speaking. And with this, the meddlesome curiosity that led me into the alley overcame whatever remaining good sense was compelling me to leave, leading me to take a few steps closer. The two men didn't seem to notice my approach, allowing me to finally pick up on what the one on the left was saying.

"I don't think you get the position you're in, lady. I don't wanna hurt ya, but you're startin' to get on my nerves."

"I will not bestow upon any mortal compensation which is not duly earned. I have no pressing desire to unleash my blade upon you, so once more I ask that you depart in peace."

The woman's voice remained firm and calm despite the apparent threat, though what really caught my attention was her use of the word "mortals". Since that was the same word Lily used to refer to humans, I had to wonder –

Could this be another spirit?

"What the hell are ya talkin' about?" The man with the hat stood up straight, revealing an intimidating height. "Just hand over what you've got, or we'll be more than happy to take it ourselves."

"My patience runs thin at this insolence. Leave now, or I will no longer stay my hand. And to think a lowly human would deign to hurl threats toward a member of the Arta...." At this point, the woman seemed to be talking to herself more than the two men standing in front of her.

"C'mon, let's just get out of here," the man on the right said. "She's clearly not all there in the head, and I doubt she's even got anything good on her. It's not worth the trouble – "

The first man brushed his partner aside and stepped forward.

"What're you afraid of? She's got nowhere to go, and it's two on one. Just help me grab her and we'll get out of here before anyone even realizes we were here."

"Uh, might be a little late for that," I muttered, shuffling closer. While my heart wanted to muster some sense of confidence, it was currently lodged in my throat.

The man on the left turned around and narrowed his eyes in frustration. "Oh, for the love of – "

Before I could react, he took a single step in my direction and threw a full punch directly into my stomach, forcing me to double over.

"The hell are you doin' getting yourself involved in something that doesn't concern you, huh?"

Still winded from that first blow, the mugger's frame loomed over me. Once again I had thrown myself into a fight with no plan and no chance of winning. I wanted to curse whatever fledgling and idiotic sense of duty had caused me to walk into this alley in the first place, but there was no time for that. Even if I didn't know what I was doing, I had to fight back. Because just like before…it wasn't my life that was at stake here. Any injuries I took, any cuts, bruises, and broken bones I walked away with – they were nothing if it meant helping someone else.

And so with no other recourse, I leapt straight up with all the strength I could muster, bringing the top of my head hard against my attacker's chin. He staggered back, gripping his jaw and letting loose a flurry of swears.

With no experience fighting (and the same amount of raw physical strength you'd expect from a perennial shut-in), I knew I wouldn't be able to win on might or tactics alone. The best I could hope for was that I could outlast them both, and that Lily's gift wouldn't let me down now.

While the first mugger was still recovering, his partner seemed to finally register what was going on and charged forward, shoulder down. There wasn't enough room to move out of the way in such a narrow space, so I threw my arms against my body and braced myself as he crashed into me. Although I was knocked off my feet, the man had left himself unbalanced as well, giving me a chance to throw a desperate flurry of punches at his side as he leaned into me, still trying to recover his footing.

This did little to deter him, however, and another fist came flying towards my head. Luckily I was able to jerk back at the last second, avoiding the full force of the blow, though the hit still connected and left me reeling, my vision going blurry. I instinctively shut my eyes and winced, expecting another surge of pain to follow suit, but nothing of the sort happened. I opened my eyes a few moments later to an almost humorous sight in front of me.

The woman I had heard speaking earlier was now holding the taller man above her head, his panicked shouts abruptly silenced as she casually tossed him on top of his partner. While me and the other mugger had been fighting, she must've somehow knocked the first one out, and then grabbed hold of the second while he was still distracted. As the woman began to readjust her clothing, brushing away a few flecks of dirt off her otherwise pristine skirt, I was at last able to get a good look at her.

Her hair was a deep gold, complemented by streaks of dark brown and tied in a braid at the top while slightly curling to the middle of her back, She wore a long, white dress, which was secured in the front by a metal chest plate. An elongated scabbard sat at her waist, as the understated yet intricately detailed handle of the sword resting within peeked out the side. Her eyes were a verdant green that did not appear to be unkind, though she had an aura that projected more steadfast determination than welcoming amicability. If nothing else, I got the feeling that her manner of speech was at least in line with how she presented herself.

"I thank you for your timely intervention, mortal, though there was scarce need for you to endanger yourself over such trivial matters," the woman said, coming forward.

"Yeah, I – I guess you're right. It kinda looks like you had everything handled yourself."

I glanced over at the limp bodies of her would-be assailants – even if they weren't the most physically intimidating men, it was pretty astounding how effortlessly she dispatched both of them. When I turned back, however, the woman had crouched down next to me, staring intently into my eyes.

"But alas, could it be…" she whispered, grabbing my face. "Yes! Providence has brought us together, as destiny did allot."

Unsure of what was going on, or even who this person was, I tried to explain the situation while my cheeks were still cradled in the woman's hands.

"Erm, I don't think we've actually met before – "

"Oh, but of course! Forgive my transgression – I have not had a chance to properly introduce myself."

The woman released me and took a step back, bowing deeply.

"I have watched you these past days, when thrice you have placed yourself in way of imminent danger, and thrice suffered greatly, all to protect another in their time of need. Whether it be through blithe ignorance of your own frailty or a heart brimming with dauntless bravery, you have garnered my attention, and so for as many days I have been seeking an audience with you."

She unlatched the leather strap running across her chest and removed the large kite shield she had been carrying on her back, dropping it on the ground with a dull crash and resting her hands atop it.

"From this day forth, I shall be your shield – your protector and stalwart comrade in the coming trials fate has set before us."

I waited for some further explanation as to who exactly she was, or what was going on in the first place, but the woman seemed perfectly content with what had already been said.

"Ok, while I'll admit that this isn't necessarily the weirdest thing that's happened to me lately," I said slowly, "I think you need to start over from the beginning. Who are you? And how exactly do you know me?"

"Ah, forgive me once more – indeed, I have not properly introduced myself, nor expounded on the nature of our encounter. If you would, allow me to elucidate."

The woman hoisted the shield to her back and approached me once more – letting me now fully appreciate just how exceptionally tall she really was, standing well over 7 feet, possibly even breaking 8 comfortably. As she had decided to stand directly in front of me, I had to crane my neck back to keep looking at her, while trying to ignore the fact that, given our height difference, my face was exactly chest-high.

At least her armor helped keep things fairly under wraps, so to speak.

"I come from the realm of heroes – an aspect of courage, if you would. I have taken it upon myself to seek out and guide those burgeoning warriors who have proven themselves as defenders of the innocent and weak."

The woman paused and bent down, so we were eye-to-eye again. Her expression softened, and she spoke with an almost nurturing tone now. "Though you may not be aware, there exist many worlds beyond the one you inhabit now. While they are largely sealed off from one another, the barriers between these other realms and your world have begun to crumble – " She looked over my shoulder at the park behind, puzzled. "At least, that much I must assume, given the sudden presence of spirits such as myself in this world."

Although everything she was saying so far seemed to indicate, beyond a shadow of a doubt, that she really was another spirit, one major question still lingered in my mind –

"What does this have to do with me?"

"...Pardon?"

"I'm...still not sure what it is you want from me."

"Ah, you see – " The woman gave an awkward smile as she let out a small laugh. "I have been searching for an appropriate candidate to swear myself to, so as to stabilize my presence in this world and, in turn, guide and train them for those battles that lie ahead. After following your most recent exploits, I am confident I have found such a vessel."

"Oh, well, um – I'm really flattered and all, but I think you might have the wrong per–"

Before I could finish, a warm sensation pressed against lips. "son."

In the next moment, a scorching sensation ran across my chest, seeming to follow the same shape as those weird markings Lily had shown me. I placed a hand over that spot, speechless, as I tried to process everything that just happened.

"The contract is sealed. I...must apologize if this agreement appears sudden, but there is little time to spare." The woman stood back up and scratched at her cheek as she looked away, her cheeks reddening. "And from what I have seen, humans seem to prefer this method of commitment."

"I – you – I – "

I struggled to form a coherent sentence as a thousand different questions rose up at once. Was this really another spirit? And had I bonded myself to her like with Lily? Was that even possible? And what kind of battles was she talking about? I wasn't any kind of fighter and –

"Look, look, just – " I took a deep breath and tried to settle my mind. "Why don't you come with me and we can get this all sorted out."

It had been a while since I left Lily alone, and I was afraid she might be getting worried. Plus, I had a feeling there was going to be quite a lot to explain to both of them.

"Ah, shall we depart for your abode then? If it be not too burdensome, I would like to share your lodgings and stay close by your side, given the uncertainty of those dangers that lurk near."

"That might – " I let out a long sigh and turned around, heading back to where I'd last seen Lily. "Yeah, fine. I'm guessing you don't have anywhere else to stay, right?"

The woman shook her head plainly.

"Alright. I'll figure something out."

I continued leading us through the park to where Lily was, as she ran over and threw her arms around me.

"Yuu! I was looking all over for you, but you were gone and – who's this?" Lily's voice dropped at this second part.

This…could be bad.

"I guess you could call her a new frien–"

The woman standing beside me cut in.

"I am his unyielding compatriot and tutor, the bearer of his shield and an extension of his will. And who, in turn, may you be?"

To my immense relief Lily appeared more confused than upset by the woman's introduction, so I took the opportunity to clarify what was going on.

"I found her in the alley over there getting harassed by two guys. I tried to help out, and, well..." I rubbed the back of my head, still aching from the previous scuffle. "Let's just say she really didn't need it. In any case, it looks like she's a spirit, same as you. And we...kind of already made a contract together."

"You did?"

I nodded hesitantly, bracing for the worst.

"That's amazing Yuu! How did you do it? Who is she? Where is she from? What did she want? Where – "

"Wait, you're not mad?"

Lily looked at me curiously. "Why would I be mad?"

"Well – "

I decided it'd be best to gloss over *how* exactly the contract was sealed.

"I-It's nothing. But since she doesn't have any other place to go, I think she might have stay with us for a while, if you're ok with that."

"Yes, yes, of course yes! It'll be like having an older sister, we can share stories, and brush each others hair, and, um – " Lily furrowed her brow in thought. "What do sisters normally do?"

"Ahem." The woman gave a light cough as she continued to stand to the side, waiting.

"Oh, right!" I nudged Lily forward, holding her in front of me. "This is Lily, my girlfriend. As you might've guessed, she's a, uh, spirit too."

The woman smiled and closed her eyes, nodding to herself in satisfaction. "It is certainly an impressive feat to have already won over the confidence of another spirit. It appears my initial assessment was not ill-founded."

"Right, so about that – you mentioned something about other spirits showing up, and that's why you're here?"

"Correct. Those forces that have ordained my presence, have likewise placed upon me the task of preventing cataclysmic disaster."

"What…kind of disaster?"

The woman looked to the sky, where dark clouds were rolling in from the tops of skyscrapers, edging towards the clearer blue and white that overhung us. "What knowledge do you posses of those worlds outside your own?"

"Not much, honestly – only whatever Lily has been able to tell me."

"I'm from the afterlife, so I don't know a lot either," she added quietly.

"You are an aspect of death? Then…" Athena seemed to become lost in her own thoughts, before shaking her head and continuing. "Never mind. Given your limited knowledge, a thorough explanation may take some time to accomplish. Shall we retire at present and continue this conversation thereafter?"

Although the storm wasn't due to hit for another hour or two, it did seem best to discuss something like this in the privacy of our own home, so the three of us began a quiet – if not somewhat tense – walk home together.

7

By the time we made it home, the streets were already darkened by the cover of rain clouds, leaving only those speckles of light streaming out of neighbors' curtains to illuminate the way. As I opened the front door and led both girls inside, a small part of me couldn't help but feel a little excited with the situation I'd stumbled into. Sure, this other woman was little more than a complete stranger, and there was no way of knowing how long either of them would stick around for, but the childish part of me wished that maybe – just maybe – it'd be for good.

Home felt a lot more like home with someone else to share it.

"Why don't we get some of the simple things out of the way first?" I suggested as we all went over to the living room. "Like what's your name? Er – if you have one?"

The woman leaned back in the sofa chair she had dropped into and looked up, nodding her head side to side. "Where I hail from, a name is earned, not given. When one has garnered the proper recognition for their prowess in battle, they are conferred a befitting moniker. Until then, we are as clay, with no identity or purpose until shaped into something more."

"But I…think we still need something to call you by, at least while you're here. Do you have a preference?"

The woman stirred in her seat, flustered. "It is near heretical to assume a name for myself, though – perhaps it would be prudent to follow the customs of this world, as you say."

She closed her eyes, thinking it over for a moment, before continuing.

"To pay homage to she from whom we all are born forth, you may call me…Athena."

"Athena, huh?" I smiled to myself and nodded. "I like that, it suits you. Oh, and I don't think I said it before, but you can call me Yuu."

The spirit's cheeks flushed once more as she fiddled with her hands. "Yes, well, I am glad you approve. However, moving on –" Clearing her throat, she quickly regained her composure. "As you are undoubtedly aware, spirits such as I and –" She paused as she looked in Lily's direction.

"Lily."

"Yes. We do not come from this world, but rather a multitude of other realms. While spirits of differing purpose have regularly communed with mortals throughout the course of their history, these relationships tend to be of a limited manner. In simplest terms, humans have maintained the favor of spirits through prayer or offering, or, in sparse circumstances, personally bonded themselves through mutual agreement."

I could feel Lily's stare boring through me.

"Bearing the mark of this covenant, they sacrifice a portion of their soul so as to allow a spirit to remain in the mortal realm. In return, the human is afforded some limited access to the spirit's abilities."

"So far that seems pretty consistent with what you've already told me, right?"

Lily nodded slowly, fixing her gaze on Athena. "Spirits from the afterlife never stay here long, and we rarely interact with beings from any of the other worlds. I'm sorry I don't know as much as – "

Before she could finish, I reached over to pat her head gently, which seemed to help set her at ease.

"It's ok, you've already been a big help. Thank you."

Lily gave a weak smile as Athena picked up where she left off.

"What worries me is the apparent and sudden influx of spirits to this realm – a thing not seen for many centuries. It is possible, however that – "

"Wait, how would you know that?" Lily asked quietly.

"How – come again?"

"How would you know something like that?" she repeated, more firmly this time.

"The world I hail from is perhaps unique in its connection to the other realms. Like a string plucked on a harp reverberates through the other chords, however subtly, so too do these changes resonate throughout the other realms, barriers or no."

"Is that why you came here?" I asked, trying to mitigate any rising tensions by keeping us on topic.

"My arrival may be greater ascribed to chance than choice," Athena murmured. "Regardless, so long as any spirits remain without a host to bind them, the rifts between your world and these infinite other realms shall widen, inviting any and all manner of being to slip through. I fear even graver calamity may ye– "

"The minotaur," Lily interrupted. Even though she was still staring at Athena, I felt this was more directed at me.

"The one at school? I – well, yeah, I guess that'd explain how it showed up all of a sudden."

"No." Lily shook her head. "That was your fault, wasn't it?"

"Me?" Athena looked taken aback. "I – "

"You can't tell me it's just a coincidence. You said you've been following him around, right?"

"Certainly he has attracted my attention on more than one occasion, yes – "

"Then it *is* your fault." Lily's voice remained even, but the gravity with which she spoke belied the emotion roiling underneath. "I didn't want to think it at first, I didn't want to believe it, but because of you…he…he got hurt. I can't – no, I won't forgive – "

"Lily, Lily – " I could hear the gentler girl slipping away, as her "other" side began to manifest again. "It's ok, I'm ok."

"But she hurt you. She could've, she – I – " Lily gradually snapped out of it and, realizing what was going on, buried her face in her hands. "I-I'm sorry, I - I didn't mean it."

I placed an arm around Lily's shoulder and squeezed her close, trying to dispel her negative feelings.

"I will admit that there is…some chance that such a creature arrived in my interim, however remote such a possibility may be," Athena said gently. At least she didn't seem too offended by Lily's sudden accusation. "But that is precisely why I have sought you out. I shall serve as your guide and protector as you seek out and bond these rogue spirits, and so close the developing rifts and maintain peace in this world."

I raised my hand once Athena finished speaking. "Question."

"Yes, of course."

"Do I get a say in any of this?"

Athena appeared genuinely confused. "What could you mean? You have already demonstrated a latent ability for attracting spirits to your side, and unwavering courage in the face of adversity. Given the gifts already offered to you, would you truly cast aside the privilege to save your land and fellow countrymen from the dangers that now befall them?"

"Well, no, I mean – maybe not. But I'm not sure I'm the right person for this kind of thing. I couldn't even protect Lily, let alone save the entire world. So shouldn't you find someone more, y'know…capable? I'm not that strong, or smart, or experienced, or – "

"Fear not, my young warrior." Athena leaned forward and grabbed my free hand, her eyes shining with a brilliant intensity. "Though all these claims may hold true, a hero yet remains locked away within your heart, yearning to burst forth on the fields of battle. With the correct tutelage, you may very well become the savior of prophecy."

I slowly pulled back, forcing a smile. "Not that I don't appreciate the, uh…high expectations you have for me, but I think you're still a little mixed up. I'm not any kind of hero. I'm – "

Lying on the ground, useless, causing more trouble than I'm worth.

"I'm just a normal, boring human. Even if I wanted to, there's no way I could do something even close to what you're saying."

"Yet you possess a unique power not of this world, do you not?"

"I don't think I – "

Athena pointed at Lily. "You have formed a contract with this spirit, correct?"

"Yeah, but – "

"Then what is the ability she bestowed upon you?"

I could see where this was going, and I hesitated to answer. Too late to turn back now, though.

"I can't die. At least, we're pretty sure that's what it is."

"And you would rather employ this for vexless leisure than endeavoring to save your fellow kind?"

"No, no – when you put it like that it sounds pretty bad, but really – "

Athena hung her head mournfully. "Truly, then? My appearance, these anomalies, is it all to be some misguided fool's errand – ?"

"Wait, wait, I, um, didn't finish," I said quickly. I didn't think she'd get so depressed over this, so the least I could do was try to humor her for the time being. "Even if I'm not the exact person you're looking for, it couldn't hurt to help out until you do find them…right?"

Athena lifted her head back up, eyes vibrant once more. Such a rapid change in mood…

"Then you consent – ?"

"Yeah – sorta. You said you want someone to make contracts with the spirits showing up in this world, right?"

"Correct."

"Then…maybe I can try to do that much. For now."

With a relieved smile, Athena stood up and offered her hand. "The path set before you will undoubtedly be harrowing, though the most valorous step is to step forth at all. I swear I will see to it that you realize the potential you still deny."

"I guess I'll be in your care the–"

I reached out to shake Athena's hand, but was stopped as Lily threw her arms around my neck, holding me back.

"Yuu can do what he wants, but…but he's still my boyfriend!"

All at once I realized how insensitive I had been up until this point. Lily and I had only been dating a few days, and already I was inviting some other woman to come live with us? Spirit or not, I couldn't blame her for feeling jealous, if not completely spurned, by the whole situation.

However, before I could utter another word, Athena spoke up. "Of course – I assure you, our relationship is distinct, and will not infringe upon the bond you two share in the slightest."

Lily relaxed her hold on me (albeit only slightly) and shook her head.

"N-no, that's not it," she said in a small voice. "I just want you to promise me something."

Athena knelt down to meet Lily's gaze. "What is it you desire?"

"You…you have to protect Yuu. He's only a human, he's – he's not like us. I don't want him to get hurt, whether he can die or not. You have to promise me, ok?"

Athena held up one hand and closed her eyes. "I swear so long as I draw breath, no harm shall befall him. I will serve as the shield to his blade; the drive to his will; the – "

"Thank you," Lily said softly. "That's…that's all I wanted to hear."

Since both girls finally seemed to be warming up to one other, we ended up spending the rest of the night swapping stories about where we came from and what our hopes for the future were. Although Lily and Athena seemed more intent on asking *me* questions than each other, I was still able to glean a little extra knowledge about them.

Lily, true to her word, had no real "family" to speak of, and apparently idled away most days without much social interaction, be it with humans or spirits. Athena, on the other hand, came from a sort of warrior academy, which sought to balance mental and physical acuity, and so seemed to have countless stories of her exploits with her own friends and instructors.

I still had a hard time believing some of the things they described – tales of enormous monsters and infinitely expansive realms were treated as nonchalantly as any other aspect of my own day-to-day life – but it was all endlessly fascinating nonetheless. I had thought that I was insulated within my own world here on Earth, and yet there were entire universes that existed far beyond even my wildest dreams. At times it was…a lot to take in, but I found my interest only grew with each new tidbit offered up. If nothing else, there was sure to be no shortage of new things for me to learn about my new housemates.

After a few more hours of chatting and serving up a quick dinner for everyone, I made my way upstairs and collapsed into bed. I had offered Lily her own separate bed multiple times, but seeing as she had already gotten used to sleeping next to me, it just became a matter of course that we shared the same sleeping quarters. Although this *technically* left more room for Athena, it wasn't like there was any kind of shortage to begin with – the house had at least five or six bedrooms (depending on how creative you wanted to be with the term), so they'd by no means be forced to share one or anything.

I glanced over to my side at Lily, who was already sleeping peacefully, her gentle, rhythmic breathing the only noticeable sound in the room.

Eh, maybe this wasn't so bad after all.

I wriggled myself further under the covers and thought about what Athena had said. It was true that Lily had given me an extraordinary gift. And I had seen firsthand how dangerous rogue monsters from these other worlds could be. It was obvious that being able to cheat death was useful in taking on things like that, but for someone like me, did that really make any difference? Sure, I couldn't be outright killed, but what good was that if I couldn't actually stop the monster from hurting anyone else? Twice now I tried to help somebody, and all I ended up doing was getting a few extra scars and bruises.

Although I would never admit it to Lily, in some way I hated myself for what she'd given me. I knew it wasn't intentional (it's not like we agreed on me gaining immortality or anything – all I wanted to do was come back to life), but it felt wrong to give a weak nobody like me such an amazing power. I couldn't even say I didn't want to use it to help people – despite what I told Athena, the idea of being someone important, of leaving some kind of positive impact on the world was an absolutely enticing.

It beat being a complete loser with no real plans for their own future, at least.

With a heavy sigh, I turned on my side, too restless to have any real chance of falling asleep. However, as I did so, my face met with a curiously soft presence. While my eyes should've adjusted to the darkened room, I still couldn't quite make out what I was pressed up against.

That, is until I heard Athena whisper a few choice words.

"Oh, are you still awake?"

"Huh? Y-yeah. Just a lot on my mind is all," I mumbled, burying my face further into whatever this cushiony presence.

…

A few seconds passed and, as the gears in my brain finally started turning, I shot up straight. Athena was lying next to me, her head propped up with one arm. This sudden movement must've woken Lily up as well, since she rubbed one eye and rolled over towards me.

"Everything ok?" she asked sleepily.

"Y-yep, everything's fine. You can go back to sleep," I said in as calm a voice as I could manage, my heart still racing. Lily gave a soft nod and tucked herself around mee, having apparently fallen back asleep right away.

Taking a deep breath, I turned back to Athen. *"Why are you here?"*

"I said I would stay always by your side, did I not? Be it day or night, I must ensure the safety of my charge."

"Look, I appreciate your concern, but I just don't think it's a great idea to share the same be–…"

My voice trailed off as Athena placed her arms around my head and pulled me back down, cradling me against her chest.

"Since the time of our founders, skinship has served to strengthen the ties between warriors." She slowly ran her fingers through my hair as she spoke, her tone gentle and motherly. "Come now, there is nothing to be ashamed of. I have shared many a more intimate embrace than this with my sisters."

I know I should've protested more, should've pulled myself away and told her to go back to her room.

As it was, however, I was comfier than I'd ever been in a very, very long time.

While Athena continued to comb my hair, my eyelids grew heavy, and sleep came upon me fast. I thought I might've heard her whisper one last thing, but at that point I was way too tired to care, as both body and mind finally gave in to a peaceful slumber.

8

I was stirred awake a few hours later by the subtle rustling of metal clattering against metal. Since it was still dark out, I couldn't see the cause of the noise, though it was easiest to chalk it up to some truck passing by outside and leave it at that. I pulled a pillow back over my head to try and fall back to sleep when –

clink clink

There it was again, closer this time. Figuring it was worth investigating now, I wearily sat up and felt around for the lamp. As I continued to fumble around in the dark, I reached a little *too* far and tumbled onto the floor with a dull thud, half my body still hanging on the bed. Brushing away a faint sense of déjà vu, I picked myself up off the ground and returned to searching for the light switch.

"Oh? Have you risen at last?" Athena's disembodied voice greeted me plainly. "Frankly I had begun to fear I would have to rouse you through some other means."

It might've been my imagination, but there was something chilling about the emphasis she placed on the word "other".

"What're you doing up so early?" I whispered. "It's not even light out yet."

Given that Athena didn't seem intent on affording Lily the

same courtesy, I'm not sure my efforts to keep my voice low meant much, but she was such a heavy sleeper it probably didn't matter either way.

More sounds of rattling metal, now paired with a brush of cloth. "Has your memory faded so soon? I informed you last night as we laid together."

"Please, don't…say it like that." It was weird enough sharing my bed with two girls I had just met; the last thing I needed were even more crude implications added on top of it. "Anyway, told me what? I must've fallen asleep before I heard you."

Athena let out something between a sigh and a laugh. "I see you were not simply being modest earlier. Very well – your training begins now."

"Wait, training? For what?"

"For the charge set out before you. You must learn to hone your martial abilities and defend yourself, so that you may maintain peace in the wake of those who would disturb it."

All at once, everything came rushing back – Athena wanted me to somehow take care of the spirits and monsters that were making their way into this world, and I relented to her pleas assuming that nothing much would come of it (at least not right away), but…here we were now.

I at last reached the lamp sitting on the nightstand and turned it on, illuminating the room in a soft glow. Athena was standing toward the center, still adjusting her chest plate over her dress, her scabbard secured back on her waist. I had to admit that I was a little taken with the aura of graceful strength she projected, a beauty equal parts intimidating as it was entrancing.

I plopped back down on the bed and continued watching her ready her armor. "So what exactly is this training all about, again?"

She grimaced and placed one hand on the hilt of her sword. "Perhaps I was too quick to pass judgment on a mortal such as yourself. Regardless, what's done is done – as my protégé, I shall shape you into a proper warrior, whatever the cost." She bent down and, grabbing me under my arms, hoisted me back to my feet. "You recall the covenant we sealed upon our first meeting, do you not?"

Thinking back on it, my mind strayed more towards the way our agreement was finalized, than the actual terms themselves; still, I got the gist of it all.

"Y-yeah, I do."

"Good. Then you must understand that, in return for the power I have bestowed upon you, you must uphold those responsibilities inherent to them." Athena paused, looking me straight in the eyes. "You have consented to binding wayward spirits to this world, and so I shall lend you the fortitude necessary to accomplish this task. However – this cannot be done through borrowed strength alone. We must also work to hone your mind and body, so that you may wield the power necessary to strike down those of evil intent."

My first instinct was to protest this growing burden, but thought better of it. I may have liked my life the way it was, despite whatever unforeseen excitement Lily brought along with her, and I could see the two of us settling into a normal life together, but I couldn't deny that – whether I wanted it or not – I had been given an exceptional gift. It seemed selfish to not at least try to put it to good use. Until I better understood what I should do with it, the least I could do was humor Athena and play along.

"Alright, alright, I'm coming. Let me just put on some clothes and – "

I moved towards the closet to at least grab a sweatshirt, but after taking a single step Athena had already taken me by the waist and threw me over her shoulder, sprinting downstairs and out of the house with surprising alacrity, given her stature and armor.

"First lesson – danger may find you at any time, and so you must always be prepared to fight, whatever the circumstances."

I stood there in the freezing early morning staring at her, stuck somewhere between confusion and frustration.

"I really don't think that's relev– "

Athena narrowed her eyes, one hand curled around her sword's grip.

"Er – never mind." I glanced around the yard, empty and spacious as it was. "What are we doing out here again?"

"First, you must acquire a weapon."

"And…how should I get one?"

Athena reached out and gently pressed her fingers against my chest, sending a tingle through my body.

"From within yourself. Search deep inside, and you will find the power you seek."

"Inside me?"

A curt nod.

"Like, in me, or – ?"

"Yes."

It was pretty clear I wasn't going to be getting any kind of clearer answer from her. So, taking a deep breath, I closed my eyes and tried to focus – on what, exactly, I wasn't sure. Athena had said to "look inside me," but for what? The motivation to fight? The kind of weapon I'd want to use? Outside of that scuffle in the alleyway, I couldn't say I'd ever been in a "real" fight before, let alone be able to imagine what sort of weapon I could use –

"Search deep *within* yourself," she repeated.

"Trying," I muttered, eyes still shut tight in concentration.

A few moments of fruitless meditation later, I heard the clinking of armor as Athena moved closer and, grabbing my hand, pressed it firmly against my chest.

"Look to the bonds you've forged and within their source – the heart itself – you will find your weapon."

I gave a quick nod and tried do as she said.

Jun and Himeo were undoubtedly my closest friends, though I wasn't sure what they had to do with any of this. And then there was Lily, of course. Even if I didn't know what I was doing as her boyfriend, I cared for her in a way I'd never felt for anyone else before. She made my heart race with that innocent smile, and, for as strange as she could be at times, she livened up each and every day. I might not fully understand my feelings for her, but I was certain I wanted to be with her. She made me happy, that much was true. Plus –

I felt Athena push against my hand again, harder this time. What was she trying to get me to do? Literally reach inside myself –

As if on cue, a burst of heat erupted in my chest, in the same place that had been marked after meeting Lily. Athena pressed even harder and, against all reason, I could feel my hand sinking in.

"Yes, that's it! Quickly now – retrieve the weapon which will allow you to forge a new path forward."

I tried to do as Athena instructed, reaching deeper inside my own body to pull out… whatever was in there. The further I went, however, the stronger the heat grew, rising to a feverish burning as I moved my wrist in. Although I was tempted to yank my hand out, I gathered my endurance and kept at it for just a few seconds longer, until my fingers finally touched upon something solid. Wrapping them around the object, I pulled with all my might and –

To my utter disbelief, I was now holding a sword in my hand. That came out of my chest. The hilt was haphazardly wrapped in worn and split leather, and the rusted, bronze blade was chipped in a number of places.

Also, it was really heavy.

Unable to hold it aloft any longer, I dropped the sword to my side, where it jutted straight into the ground. Looking up at Athena, I could see that she bore the slightest hint of a smile.

"I will confess, you have exceeded my expectations." She unrooted the sword and held it up to her eyes, examining it closely. "Not the finest weapon, but it should suffice for now."

She tossed the sword back to me, which I fumbled a bit before dangling it by the hilt.

"This weapon is an extension and a reflection of you – know it well. As it is pulled from your heart, so too does it mirror your soul."

"Then this…this really came from inside me?" I glanced at the sword held limp by my side, still trying to come to terms with what happened. "I mean, Lily showed me that she can make a scythe out of her ribbon, but she's a spirit, so that's one thing. I'm just a normal human, so it's not like – "

Athena placed a finger to my lips and shook her head. "The bond between spirit and mortal elevates both beyond what they once were. Neither are solely tied to their place of origin, and so neither are limited by the rules of their respective realms." She took my hands in hers and wrapped them tight around the hilt, lifting the sword into the air. "Only through the bonding of spirit and mortal can the true potential of a soul be tapped. You would do well to remember that."

She took a step back, as if to admire her handiwork, leaving me to try to hold the weapon steady on my own again. Of course my arms gave out after only a few seconds, suggesting that either it was unnaturally heavy, or I was pathetically weak.

…

For the sake of not obliterating my own ego, I decided to go with the first option.

Athena looked from me to the sword (now resting back on the ground) and tilted her head. I prepared myself for her inevitable disappointment but, surprisingly, she seemed more curious than anything.

"I see we must first train your body before even considering the basics of combat." She nodded to herself and took a step forward. "Very well – to exercise the body is to establish a firm foundation upon which we will mold you into a warrior. Let us begin."

And with that, Athena kicked my legs out from under me, leaving me lying face-first on the ground.

"We'll begin with yours arms. Go."

Under her watchful gaze, and without really thinking, I began to do as many push-ups as I could, which was…not many. Any time I seemed to be reaching my limit, however, Athena grabbed me by the collar and pulled me back up, insistent that I keep going. After repeating this same routine six or seven times, my arms stopped responding altogether, which appeared to satisfy her at last.

"Given it is your first day, we should take it easy and halt there."

"That…was taking it…*easy*?" I choked out, staggering to my feet. "At least…you're being…merciful – "

"Now let us move on to stamina training."

Spoke too soon.

Athena pushed me forward past the fence that separated the backyard from the adjacent road, goading, chiding – and eventually threatening – me into jogging until my legs could take no more.

My heart practically bursting out of my chest, each breath coming out as a desperate, wheezing gasp, I fell to the ground, unable to move even if my life really did depend on it. Athena must've finally been convinced that I couldn't take any more, as she threw me back onto her shoulder and carried me the rest of the way home.

I suppose I had to be thankful for that small courtesy, at least.

By the time we made it back to the house, Lily had already gotten up and was waiting for us in the kitchen, though she still seemed to be half-asleep, resting her head on the table. When she heard the back door slide open, she offered us a sleepy greeting and asked where we were. I could only offer a tired groan in response as I limped over to the chair next to Lily, so Athena answered in my place.

"His first day of physical training began this morning."

I collapsed into a chair next to Lily and slumped over.

"There is…still quite some work to be done. Though I can assure you that each challenge you surmount lessens the next you may face."

I gave a small nod, resting my head on the table.

I had no idea if my body could actually hold up to this kind of regimen, but I had a feeling that there would be little use in trying to argue with Athena. Given how "insistent" she showed she could be be, I was fairly certain that, no matter what I said or did, she'd still find a way to get me to keep up with it, so I might as well save myself the trouble and try my best. Plus, it wouldn't kill to me get some real exercise for once.

I, uh…hoped.

Either way, with a somewhat renewed resolve, I pushed myself away from the table and set about making breakfast. I didn't think spirits would have the same kinds of needs as humans, but as Athena had explained earlier, spirits who are bonded to the human world take on some of its physical traits, becoming a little more like mortals themselves, needing to eat, sleep, and so on. I began to think about what it must be like to suddenly have needs you'd never known before, when I heard Lily start to mumble.

"W-wait, training for what?"

She…wasn't the quickest to the draw in the morning.

"As we discussed last night, Yuu has agreed to seal those wayward spirits that make their way into this realm. However, in order to protect himself while doing so, he must learn to fight."

Lily sat up, fully alert now, and turned towards Athena. "But…does he really have to do that? He's just a hu– "

"It is the desire of every true warrior to fight for those who cannot defend themselves, to find glory in battle and to secure victory through whatever challenges laid before them. Likewise – " She glanced in my direction. "He has agreed to this contract by his own volition. His reasons for doing so remain his own, though he holds an obligation nonetheless to honor it."

For a moment, no one said anything. Like the start of an avalanche, I could see disaster on the horizon, but had no way to stop or avert it. And so, rather than jump in now, I decided to wait for an opportune time to say my piece, hoping that I wouldn't incite an even worse argument than what was broiling now.

"And what if he doesn't?" Lily asked quietly.

"Come again?"

"What if he doesn't do what you want?" she repeated.

"I see no reason why he should deny it, given his prior agreement – "

"Did you even ask him?" Lily's voice remained calm, though the anger hiding behind the even tone was plain to see. "Did you even ask him if this is what he wants?"

"O-of course," Athena murmured, patting down the creases in her dress. "He can tell you himself, correct?"

Both girls now directed their attention to me.

"I - well, you see – "

I really had no idea what to say. If I lied and said I was all for helping Athena out, I'd no doubt make Lily feel like I didn't need her or – worse yet – was trying to replace her. But if I admitted that I still wasn't sure about fulfilling the contract, I might irreparably harm my relationship with Athena; considering that she was as much a stranger to this world as Lily, and so had no one else to go to, I wanted to avoid that, too.

Thankfully (or not), Lily intervened before I could stammer out any kind of half-hearted concession.

"Yuu, can you tell me one thing?" She leaned in close, watching me intently.

"Y-yeah, anything."

"Did you actually agree to make a contract with her?"

"Why would y– " Athena tried to protest, but Lily quickly

silenced her.

"Let him answer."

"I guess – " Further into the minefield I waded. "I can't say I did at first, at least not in the traditional way. But now that – "

Lily slammed her hands on the table and rose up. "Then you tricked him!"

"I did no such thing – !"

"Shut up!" At last, Lily's voice began to quaver as tears welled up in her eye. "He didn't even know who you were! You just showed up out of nowhere and forced him…forced him to work for you. If he meets other spirits, fine. But why are you making him fight? Why? Do you really not care what he thinks, what he wants – "

"If I recall correctly, you forged your own contract in exchange for his revival, did you not?"

Although Athena towered over Lily, she stood defiant, fixing her gaze on Athena.

"You – "

"I humbly request that, before you cast accusations upon others, you might reflect on the nature of your own actions."

Athena smiled, though there was no happiness behind it.

"Or do you truly think your union is of pure passion? Perhaps you do not want to acknowledge the truth that lies – "

"Athena, that's en– "

"I don't know what you want…" Lily whispered, hanging her head. "I don't know where you really came from, or who you really are. I don't know what you think you're doing barging in on us out of nowhere, and acting like you understand even the tiniest little bit about us. You don't know me, or him, or us." Lily lifted her face, tears streaming down her cheek.

"Lily, I – " I reached out to touch her shoulder, but she

brushed my hand away.

"Who are you, really? What is it you want?" She pushed against Athena, though she didn't budge. "We were happy together. We've *been* happy together! Things would have been fine if you hadn't shown up."

Throughout this rant, Athena remained stoic as ever.

"Why won't you say anything? What are you hiding? Why are you even here? No one asked you to be here! At least I came here because he wanted to be with me – what's your excuse?" Lily paused and, when no response was forthcoming, nodded to herself. "That's what I thought."

She walked away from the table, the sound of her light footsteps only brought to an end by the slamming of the bedroom door upstairs.

"Goddammit…"

I sunk back into my chair, defeated.

No matter how you looked at it, this was entirely my fault. I thought things might be ok since Lily and Athena had a chance to get to know each other better last night, but it was naïve to think that their differences would be so easily resolved. I mean, I never even told Lily what had happened when I met Athena, nor did I tell either of them explicitly how I feel about the whole situation myself – given that I was their only real connection to this world, I couldn't blame them for getting upset when there was still so much they didn't know about my own feelings.

As I debated whether I should go and see Lily now or give her more time to cool off, I felt a hand lightly tap on my shoulder.

"I…did not mean to cause you distress," Athena said quietly, looking away. "I do not know what came over me, though I understand that my behavior was unbefitting of both a mentor and guest. I would like – " She folded her hands and bowed deeply. "To humbly ask your forgiveness."

"No, it's – " I reached over and awkwardly patted her on the back, causing her to stand up straight again. "It's fine, really. And I should be the one apologizing, anyway."

Athena looked surprised. "What need is there for you to do so?"

"I've kind of gone along with everything you've been asking me to do, without being totally honest about how I feel."

I shifted in my seat, trying to shake out some of the lingering soreness.

"I don't disagree with you that what Lily's given me is an amazing power, and could be used to help a lot of people. In fact – "

I felt my chest tighten as all the ways I'd made a fool of myself in the past few days ran through my mind.

"Before any of this happened, I wasn't really doing anything with my life. So I think there's a part of me – maybe just a small part, but I won't say it's not there – that's excited by the thought of being someone important. Or at least doing something that matters."

"Then why – "

"Because I'm scared."

Athena knelt down so that we could speak face-to-face. Her eyes, though still unfamiliar, held an endless supply of contradictions – gentle yet domineering, nurturing yet harsh, amicable yet distant. Whereas Lily tended to wear her emotions on her sleeve, Athena was much harder to read.

"Then what is it you fear?"

"Losing both of you. Getting others hurt. Not – "

You're only a human.

"Not being strong enough to protect the people most important to me."

"That is the reason you must train – "

I shook my head. "What if that's not enough? Even if – " I
knew it was ridiculous to say this, but I had to be honest. "Even
if we only just met, it already feels like you're an important
part of my life. I don't want to put you or Lily in harm's way
because – "

Athena reached over and pulled my face close to her chest,
my cheek pressed against the cool metal of her breastplate as
she pet my head gently.

"There, there…" she cooed. "Is that truly all that plagues
you?"

"I…I guess so."

I felt her body shift slightly as she moved herself closer. "May
I share with you a small piece of wisdom given to me by my
own sister?"

"Yeah, please." I tried to focus on her words despite the
ridiculous pose I was now in, pulled halfway over the back of
the chair and pressed against her armor.

"All strength is born of fear, all courage of weakness. It is
not those of iron heart who claim victory through adversity,
but rather she who fights from within what would restrain
her." Athena let go of my face and looked down at the palm
of her hand. "Regardless, it was perhaps – no, certainly is –
improper to heave upon you such a responsibility without your
full consent. Though there are…worries yet I carry with me –
"

It sounded like there was more she wanted to say, but before
I could ask about it, she had already moved on.

"If you should wish it, I will dissolve our contract and

aggrieve you no longer."

"No, I – "

I paused and looked into Athena's eyes again. She had come to this world knowing no one and with no idea how she got here, and yet she had still put her faith in me. There was no reason to think she was trying to take advantage of me, or that I was really the "best" candidate for this job.

No – Athena chose me because she was scared, and alone, and needed someone to rely on. I couldn't turn my back on her now.

"I want you to stay. And I want to help you the best I can. Not because of any obligation, but because…because you're my friend."

Athena stared at me for a moment, before letting out an incredulous laugh. "You truly are a strange creature, though…"

Finally, an honest smile spread across her lips.

"That is what I find most endearing about you. Now go – you've idled long enough speaking to me, while another still waits."

"Yeah, you're right."

With my own half-hearted smile, I gingerly got to my feet and made my way upstairs to where Lily had secluded herself. I approached the bedroom door and gave it a few light knocks to let her know I was there.

"Hey, Lily? Can I come in?"

Through the faint rustling of sheets I heard a muffled "Mhm", and so slowly cracked open the door. Lily was lying down on the bed, curled up in a ball with her face buried against the pillows. I felt terrible for leaving her like this, but I knew that she probably needed a little time to herself first.

"Are you doing alright?" I asked as I stepped inside.

The pillows shifted up and down, which I took as her consent.

"Then can I talk to you for a bit?"

The same movement seemed to indicate another "Yes".

I walked over to the bed and sat down on the edge, next to the covered lump that was my girlfriend. "I…wanted to apologize for what Athena said back there, and for not talking things over with you first. Even though I never planned to contract with another spirit, I should've taken the time to tell you more about it."

I ran my hand along the sheet, the worn texture having taken on a new significance in recent days.

"It may be a little late, but I was hoping I could do that now."

"Mm."

"When I first ran into Athena yesterday, I…didn't actually know who she was, either. I didn't even know she was a spirit at first."

"Really?" Lily's voice was still muted as she talked into the pillow, but I could more or less make out what she was saying.

"Yeah. I saw some strangers in an alleyway, and before I even knew what was going on, I was trying to save her from being mugged. Though to be honest – " I let out a pained laugh. "I was the one who ended up needing to be rescued again. Still, the next thing I knew, I was already bound in another contract. I can't say it's not my fault, but…"

I was fairly certain I understood what was bothering Lily, but I wanted to treat it with appropriate tact.

"I guess what I'm trying to say is, I want you to know I'd never try to replace you. I really, really do like you, and, contract or not, I want to be your boyfriend."

Slowly, Lily wriggled towards me and wrapped her arms

around my middle. "Do you mean it?"

"I do."

"Then say it again."

"I like you?"

She squeezed tighter, sending a fresh chill through my body. "Again."

"I like you."

"Again."

"I like you," I said, laughing softly as I ran my fingers through her hair.

Lily rose up and pressed her nose to mine, smiling peacefully. "I like you too, Yuu. I always have."

"So…no hard feelings?"

"No, no, it was nothing like that," she said quietly, shaking her head. "I wasn't mad at you, really. It's just…I don't know what I'd do if something happened to you."

"You're the one who told me I can't die though, right?"

"I know, I know, but you can still be hurt – no, you *have* been hurt.

She grabbed my hand and pulled it close to her, as if it was a protective charm.

"So when you started talking about fighting, and battle, and – and – " Lily struggled to choke back the tears welling up once more. "I don't want to see you in pain. I don't want to see you bleeding. I don't – I don't want that…"

"I can't promise you nothing bad will happen while we're together," I said gently, bringing her closer. "And I'm most afraid that if I let you down again, this time you'll be the one who's hurt."

"No! You – "

"Like you said, I'm only human. There's a lot I can't do,

and there's so much I still don't understand about spirits and monsters and the other worlds and all that. If I keep putting myself in situations I'm not prepared for, I risk hurting a lot more people than only me."

"No, I didn't mean it like that!" Lily said, distraught. "It's just…I mean – "

"Shh, I know, I know." I patted her head and tried to offer a reassuring smile. "But it's not bad to recognize my own shortcomings. And up until now, I've been way too indecisive. So when you're ready, can you come back downstairs? There's something I want to say to you and Athena."

"Mhm, there's something I want to say to her, too. Just – " Lily nestled her head against my shoulder, her dark hair tickling my chin. "Let me stay like this a little longer. Let me know I'm really here."

I wrapped my arm around her back and tightly embraced her. The only words I could say could never match the words in my heart, so I stayed silent as I held her. For now, that was enough.

* * *

A few minutes later and we decided it was best not to keep Athena waiting, returning to the first floor together. As we came around the corner, I saw that Athena was still in the kitchen, pacing back and forth.

"Hey, we're back."

"Oh, hello – " As soon as she took notice of Lily, Athena froze up. "Um, and to you, too."

"Hi," Lily said softly.

"I…wish to apologize for my previous transgressions. My

actions were rash, and my words piercing – I hope that you may forgive me, and pay them no further mind."

"No, I was the one who started it in the first place. You…" Lily went up to Athena, craning her neck so she could still see her. "You really care about Yuu, don't you?"

Athena blushed fiercely and began to stammer. "W-well c-certainly I should expect that there is some manner of care from a teacher towards their pupil, so you see – "

Lily giggled and threw her arms around Athena. "Even if you talk funny, I understand. We really aren't that different."

Athena gave me a desperate look, but all I could do was motion for her to return the affection. Seeing no other option, she carefully placed her arms over Lily's shoulders, who peeked her head away to speak again.

"You really do promise not to let anything happen to him?"

Athena closed her eyes and nodded. "I swear that so long as he is in my charge, no harm shall befall him."

Satisfied, Lily hugged Athena once more. "Thank you. If…if he has to fight, then at least I know you'll look out for him."

"I'm glad to see you two are friends again," I said. "There's actually something I need to say to both of you as well."

The two spirits turned their attention back to me, as Lily still clung to Athena.

"I've decided I'll do what I can to help take care of whatever spirits and monsters show up. I don't know how much that really is, but I want to give it my all. Athena, Lily – " I looked to each of them in turn. "I'll be counting on both of you, if that's ok."

Both girls sidled over and added me to the group hug, a mixture of warmth and frigidity emanating from either side.

"I shall protect and guide you," Athena said.

"And I'll always be right here, by your side," Lily seconded.

Although I had no way of knowing the grave danger I'd soon bring us into, in that moment – if only for a moment – I felt truly safe.

9

About a week had passed since meeting Athena, and although (true to her word) training only intensified each day, I was at least starting to get a little more accustomed to it. Sure, she had to practically (or in some cases, literally) drag me out of bed each morning, and by the end of most sessions I was certain I'd never be able to lift my arms again, but I was gradually adapting to the rigors of daily exercise – each push-up, each mile ran, each swing of the sword became just a little easier with practice.

In addition, things had been fairly peaceful both at home and over in the city – Lily and Athena were slowly growing closer, having found that there was more they could relate to than they first thought (what with both being spirits and indefinite residents of the human world), and there hadn't been any major reports due to "otherworldly activity" (as we'd taken to calling it) nearby. Likewise, the school had finished up its repairs in a remarkably short amount of time, so things were finally settling back into some sense of normalcy, even if I knew deep down it couldn't last.

Still, going back to school was nice in a way, considering that I hadn't seen either Jun or Himeo since classes were suspended. As I passed the front gate and tried to mentally prepare myself for the day ahead, I ran a hand across my abdomen, feeling the outline of a thick scar through my jacket, running from side to stomach. I felt a small bit of relief knowing that it was in a place no one was likely to see, and thus wouldn't be inclined to ask about it.

I knew no one would believe me if I told them what I had actually seen back then – despite everything, I still had trouble believing it myself at times – so discretion was the better part of honesty. Plus, there were a lot of unanswered questions with regard to Rick and whatever supposed government organization he worked for; I wouldn't necessarily say he was a bad guy, but he didn't give off the most trustworthy vibes, either. Because of that, I decided it'd be best to keep Athena's presence a secret. If Rick ever did find out about her...

Well, we'd cross that bridge when we got there.

Though the rest of the day was blissfully uneventful, I wandered through most of it in a complete haze, as some persistent sense of anxiety hung over me. Even as I tried to clear my mind and focus on what the teachers were saying, my thoughts kept returning to what happened here only a week or so ago. Sure, at the time Lily was able to step in before anyone else got seriously hurt, but would I always be that lucky? I know I agreed to train with Athena for this very reason, but it was hard to cast off my doubts that I would ever be able to stand up to something like that, in this lifetime or any other.

Because of this, I jumped at Jun's suggestion that the four of us (Lily having been welcomed as a regular member of our little group) go out to a local café to catch up. Since club activities were still suspended for the rest of the week, and Jun wasn't needed at his work today, we had been gifted a rare chance to spend some time together outside of school. I held on to the small hope that getting out of my own headspace might help take my mind off things for a while, as well.

I had wanted to invite Athena to come with us, but she had already agreed to stay behind and watch the house during the weekdays – between her somewhat esoteric way of speaking and the fact that she looked significantly more...*mature* than a high school student, she would've had a much harder time blending in than Lily. I felt guilty leaving her alone for most of the day, but she found a number of ways to occupy her time – for example, despite her occasionally severe tendencies, she had picked up an immediate interest in gardening. After showing her what a pitiful state of disrepair the backyard garden (now no more than a few stray stones sectioning off a patch of dirt and weeds) had fallen into, she vowed with the fervor of a true warrior to "see it bloom with a floral beauty destined to rival that of the gods' own estate".

At least I couldn't fault her for a lack of enthusiasm.

Himeo, Jun, Lily, and I went over to the café right as the sky was taking on amber shades; with winter getting ever closer, the evenings crept up even faster. The store itself was a casual place, with its own mish-mashed style that made it stand among the many other similar establishments. The stone exterior inset against the surrounding buildings gave the impression of a small, almost rustic building, similar to the bakery me and Lily went to before, though the interior was comparatively expansive, allowing plenty of room for customers to spread out, and even be afforded some semblance of privacy.

None of us could be considered "regulars" at this place, but the few times we were all able to go we thoroughly enjoyed the experience, so it sort of naturally became our de facto meetup spot. Between the light music playing through staticky speakers in the corner, to the give of the seat's padding that showed they were well-loved, to the way that the one hostess we always saw felt more like an old family friend than a complete stranger, it was the kind of place where time seemed to stop, if only for a few minutes, so you could relax and forget the world.

Or…something like that.

We scouted out a table in a less-busy part of the café and sat down, me and Lily on one end and Jun and Himeo on the other, as Jun continued going over his next plan to win the heart of some girl he had set his sights on – I couldn't be sure (this was a regular occurrence regardless of the time of year), but odds were that with the lunar festival coming up, he was getting slightly desperate for a date.

I was happy to wish him the best, but, given his uncanny ability to win individuals of any gender over (whether through charisma or sheer perseverance), he probably didn't need it. The fact that this ultimately led to more than a few broken hearts over the years was never something that never seemed to bother him much, though, to be fair, very little ever did.

"So – " Jun began anew, having finished up explaining how the need for tutors in light of the upcoming final exams would afford the perfect opportunity to, I quote, "get closer to my pick of the litter". I offered a silent prayer for those poor girls who fell for him, one way or another. "What've you two been up to lately? I saw you run out of the classroom last week, but after the whole school evacuated neither of us could find you."

"We were worried that something might've happened to you, at least until we got word that there were no injuries. Why did you even go out there in the first place?" Himeo asked, rolling a straw wrapper between her fingers. She had a habit of distracting herself when trying to be direct with anything approaching affection towards me or Jun.

"Oh, uh, sorry about that," I said sheepishly. "We just wanted to check out what was going on, and originally planned to head back to the classroom right away. But by the time we finished looking around the hallway, we heard the announcement telling everyone to leave, so we must've gotten out of there just before you guys."

"Well, all's well that ends well, right?" Jun flashed a grin and shook Himeo playfully, who seemed slightly less amused with the whole situation. "Plus, can't exactly complain about a few days off."

"Yeah, I guess you're right – " Himeo murmured.

"*WAIT*," Jun proclaimed. "Say that again?"

"Say what again?"

"You said I was r – i – g – h – t. A first, ladies and gentlemen!" Jun swept his hand across the table in a grand display.

"A broken clock is right twice a day, and an idiot once a lifetime," Himeo responded flatly, though a subtle smirk belied the true nature of her jab. "Anyway, Lily – "

She jumped to attention upon hearing her name called. "Hm? Yes?"

"I hope Yuu hasn't kept you cooped up this whole time, has he? I know he doesn't go out much, so – "

"No no no!" Lily waved her hands frantically. "Yuu's been taking me to all kinds of new places whenever he can. It really feels like there's always something new to see or do together."

I smiled to myself at Lily's explanation, happy that she was enjoying her time here, and relieved that she'd gotten better about not mentioning things related to spirits or the other realms.

"There's still so much I need to learn about this world, and yet it's hard to believe it's always changing like this…"

…For the most part.

"What about you two?" I asked, trying to move the conversation along before anyone noticed her strange phrasing. "Do anything fun lately?"

"Mostly working on the student council," Himeo sighed. "It's not that I don't enjoy helping plan for school events, but I wish so much of the work didn't still fall to us. It's like – " She waved her hand in the air. "It's like, every other club hates us for what we ask them to do, but if they put in just a little bit of extra work, it'd make everything else go so much smoother."

"Whatdya mean?" Jun asked, flagging down the server for another drink.

"Well…" Himeo glanced in his direction. "If I didn't have *someone* running around telling all the other clubs not to file their paper work, I wouldn't have to hunt down each president and force them to fill it out personally."

"Oh come on, somebody's gotta force you out of that tiny office every now and then. A good student president should get to know the school in person! And anyway – " Jun's voice became hushed. "Don't you think it's a little ridiculous how many forms you have to file? If enough of the other clubs speak up about it, maybe the administration will actually listen – "

"And come complaining to me," Himeo finished for him. "I know you want to help, but please, for my sake, try to help a little less."

"Fine, fine," Jun said with a dismissive wave. "At least it'll all be worth it when we go to the festival."

He paused and looked to me.

"You are still going, right?

"Yes, yes, I am." I felt a tug on my sleeve. "We both are. You have my word." Lily nodded vigorously in affirmation.

Ever since I had mentioned it to her, Lily had been pleading for me to take her to the festival. Not a day went by without her asking – just to be super duper, absolutely, completely, entirely sure – that I would bring her with me. Not like I could blame her for it; the event was big enough to draw in visitors from other nearby cities, so I couldn't imagine what it was like for someone from an entirely different world.

"I've never gotten to go to something like that, and, um…" Lily looked down at the table as she fidgeted in her seat. "I heard someone at school say that if you go with the person you love, you'll be sure to stay with them forever."

She looked to me with an expression more serious than such a silly rumor perhaps warranted.

"So we have to go, ok?"

"We will, we will, don't worry." I ruffled Lily's hair as she giggled and shook my hand off.

I had to admit that I was starting to get a little excited as well – it certainly wasn't the kind of event where you *needed* to have a date, and, for someone like me, that always seemed like a far-flung fantasy in the first place. So the prospect of actually getting to go with a girl – my bona fide girlfriend, no less – was thrilling in its own way.

"I'm glad someone's looking out for him," Himeo teased. "Make sure he keeps his word and treats you well, ok?"

"Yes!"

Satisfied, Himeo turned her attention back to Jun, who was resting his head on his hand and staring off at the wall. She poked him in the cheek as she spoke. "Hey, why so quiet all of a sudden?"

"Hm? Me?" Jun spoke like he was coming out of daze.

"Uh, yeah you. What's up? It's not like you to be so out of it."

"Ah sorry, there's just a lot on my mind right now." He shook his head and forced a smile. "Anyway, it's kind of a shame Yuu's already taken, I could've used a wingman for the festival – I'm sure he could've even picked up a cutie himself if he put his mind to it."

Remembering who was present, he glanced at Lily.

"Not to imply anything, of course."

"What about that first-year you were talking about asking out?" I asked.

"Ah! Ever the sharp memory, Mr. Risher," Jun said with renewed energy, pushing up his glasses. "As I always say: Sometimes a plan, always a back-up."

"That…doesn't make any sense – "

"Nor does any matter of the heart! Lily – "

"Huh? I – me?" Lily was still getting used to Jun's rapid transitions. Then again, so was I.

"How do you know you love your boyfriend?"

"I-I'm not sure," she stammered. "I'm not even sure what it is – "

"Say no more, say no more," Jun interrupted, holding out his hand. "A maiden's feelings are as much a mystery to herself as they are to any other."

"And your point being?" I asked.

"There is no sense in attempting to account for all the ways a romantic inclination may weave and wane, and so I devote as little energy as possible to it. Think about it: which is more compelling – a calculated arrangement decided upon because it would be mutually beneficial for both parties, or a sweeping and intimate confession made on a heart's whim?"

I winced at this unintentional indictment.

"The...second one, I guess."

"Precisely!" Jun slapped his hand down on the table. "The wise man plans his steps – but the smart man knows his destination."

"What are you even talking abou– "

"It's all well and good to have a plan, however – " He tapped the rim of his glasses with a smirk. "No plan is destined to work the way you think it will. So rather than act beholden to them, I simply assume that whatever ideas I have *won't* work out, and always prepare to make it up as I go along. The greatest passions bloom in the spur of the moment, after all."

"You know, that'd almost be admirable if you weren't such a philandering dummy," Himeo cut in, pushing Jun towards the edge of the booth. "Anyway, scooch. You reminded me that I need to have a little one-on-one girl time with Lily, so I'll leave you both to talk about whatever for a bit."

She smiled at Lily and held out her hand.

"You don't mind coming with me for a little, right?"

Lily looked to me with concern, hesitating as she stepped out of the booth. "Don't worry, I'm not going anywhere." I nudged her forward as she grabbed Himeo's hand, following her toward the restroom.

Jun propped one elbow on the table and watched the two girls until they turned the corner, out of sight and earshot. "You ever wonder what they talk about in there?"

"Horrible and arcane secrets not suitable for male ears, probably."

Jun nodded thoughtfully and continued staring into the distance, resting his head on his hand. He seemed to be lost in thought again, so I decided to keep quiet, not wanting to interrupt. After a minute or two, however, Jun broke the silence.

"Hey, Yuu." He spoke without turning his head towards me. "Can I ask you something?"

"Yeah, of course. What's up?"

"What's really going on with you and Lily?"

I felt a small chill run down my back.

"W-what do you mean?"

"You're not the kind of person to hide things, at least not from us. Himeo didn't want to pry, but I know – we both know – there's something weird going on with you two." He leaned forward, glancing to the side. "I mean, I know you'd tell us if you were dating someone - *especially* if they were coming to live with you all of a sudden. I've been your friend for long enough to know that's just not the kind of thing you'd do."

I didn't say anything at first, only watched Jun's expression – concern, pain, curiosity all rolled into one – and tried to think of some way to explain it all.

"It's…complicated," I said carefully. "There's a lot I've been wanting to tell you, and I planned to from the start, but - but I'm not sure you'd believe me."

Now it was Jun's turn to be surprised. With a small chuckle he raised one eyebrow and shook his head. "I already know you have a girlfriend, so I kind of doubt you could tell me anything more unbelievable than that."

"Fine, fine." I really did feel bad keeping everything a secret from Jun, and I figured if anyone was inclined to believe me, it'd be him. "Then, do you…believe in ghosts?"

"…What?"

"Just tell me. And be honest."

Jun must've been able to tell that I was being completely serious with this inquiry, as he sat back and thought it over. "I dunno. I feel like there's not enough proof for me to say that I do, but I guess whether I believe in them or not doesn't change the reality of their existence."

"Right, right…"

Maybe this wouldn't be so bad after all.

"So, you know how Lily's not from around here, right?"

Jun nodded slowly.

"I don't know how I should put it, but she's from…far away."

"Yeah?" He tilted his head to the side, still confused. "I don't see why that'd be such a big deal. She might say some weird things every now and then, but I'd expect that from anyone who's not from around here. If that's all you were worried about – her fitting in and all – you should've just said so from the start – "

"No, no – " I closed my eyes, trying to think how I could possibly explain this in an even semi-logical way. "When I say she's from far away, I mean *really*, *really* far away. Like, a-different-world far away."

Jun narrowed his eyes, possibly trying to figure out if I was just making a bad joke or had completely lost it.

"Are you feeling ok?" he asked at last.

"No, I mean – yes, I'm fine." I let out a brief sigh, feeling defeated. "Trust me, I know how insane this all sounds, but it's the truth. Lily isn't a human, and she isn't from Earth."

"So what are you saying? She's like…an alien or something?"

"No, no, nothing like that, it's – let me start from the beginning."

I went over with Jun what I could remember about dying and meeting Lily, us fighting the minotaur together, talking to Rick and finding out about his organization, and how I had found (and was now living with) yet another spirit.

"And there you have it," I said, finishing up my brief review. "I…probably sound ridiculous to you."

Jun sat quiet for a moment. "You do. I mean, if anyone else had told me even half of what you just said, I would've thought they were just some superstitious weirdo looking for attention. But – " He shook his head. "I can't think of a single reason why you'd try to lie about this. So even if I don't believe it all myself, I'll believe in you."

"Thanks, really." I smiled slightly, relieved. "It feels good to finally be able to talk to someone about this. Though I guess I should tell Himeo sometime, as well – "

"Tell me what?" As if on cue, Himeo had come back with Lily, retaking their respective seats in the booth.

"Oh, uh, it's kind of a long story, and – "

"Shot in the dark here – that Lily is a spirit?"

I swiftly looked from one girl to the other, though all I got in return were a pitying look and confident smirk.

"Yeah - I - but…how did you know?"

Himeo giggled and pointed at Lily. "C'mon, you think I didn't realize something was up after the first time we met? Give me a little more credit than that."

She stuck out her tongue teasingly and continued.

"When I was helping Lily at the store, she told me all about herself, including where she really came from. I'll admit, I wasn't sure what to think at first, but just look at this face –" She reached over and put her hands around Lily's cheeks. "I don't think she could lie like that even if she wanted to. That's why I pulled her away earlier – we were going to explain the whole situation, but it seems you beat me to it."

"But…but if you already knew, why didn't you say something sooner?"

Himeo shrugged. "I figured that if you didn't want to tell me right away, then you were trying to keep it a secret for whatever reason. Plus, couldn't I say the exact same thing to you?"

"Alright, point taken." I nodded at Himeo and Jun in turn. "I'm sorry for hiding all this from both of you for so long. I just really wasn't sure how to bring it up, and I didn't want you thinking I was crazy or anything."

Jun stretched back and looked to the side, watching a small trickle of other customers mill about by the bar. "Like I said, I'm still not sure I believe this all myself, but – real or not – if something's bothering you, you can talk to us. You should know that much."

"You're right, you're right – I should've trusted you all more." I met Lily's hand with mine and squeezed. "Thanks guys. And…ditto. I may not be good for much, but I'm always here for you, too."

"At least you acknowledge it," Jun said casually.

I shot a glare in his direction. "Wait, what's that supposed to mean?"

"Nothing. Just saying – I'm always the one who has to get us out of trouble, y'know?"

"You're always the one to get us *into* trouble in the first place!"

"Hey, hey, hey, I resent that! Without me – "

"My life would be a lot more peaceful, yes."

"*Boring*, you mean to say. If I didn't get you out of your house every now and then, I swear you'd never see the light of day."

This argument may have continued, but my attention was brought back to Lily as she tugged on my sleeve again.

"Yuu?" she said softly. "Can I ask you something too?"

"Huh? Y-yeah, go ahead."

"Do you think...other people will accept me for what I am, too?"

The table fell silent at Lily's question.

I think we all knew, in one way or another, that not everyone Lily met would be so understanding about her unique background. It wasn't hard to imagine those that didn't believe her thinking she was just delusional, and those that *did* thinking she was some kind of monster or freak.

"That's, uh, difficult to say. There's a lot of people in the world, and I'm not sure all of them will be as nice as Jun and Himeo are. But – " I met her gaze and offered a full, genuine smile. "Those people don't matter. And even if it takes a long time, I'm sure they'll come around someday. We just have to be patient."

"Someday..." Lily smiled faintly. "When that happens, I want to stand with you, right there in front of all of them, and tell them what I really am – "

She paused and shook her head.

"No, *who* I really am."

"Yeah." I placed my other hand on top of Lily's.

No matter how long, no matter the cost –

"I'll always stay by your side."

10

"Say again?"

During what had been an otherwise lazy evening, Athena burst into my room while I was going over some notes at my desk in the corner.

"I said, I believe we should go on a d– " She stopped herself mid-sentence. "An excursion of sorts. Together."

She seemed flustered for some reason, looking away at the wall as she talked. Given the authority and confidence with which Athena usually spoke, I had to admit it was a little funny to see this less-refined side of her.

"Sure, I mean - that sounds like fun. But, uh, why so sudden?"

Athena appeared to get even more agitated by this question, grabbing on to the hem of her skirt and tugging at it listlessly.

"Given what she said, at times brazenness takes the triumph of forethought..." she muttered.

"What do you – "

"Nothing, nothing." She shook her head and continued. "You must surely understand my intentions - since I have joined you, I have not been afforded the opportunity to converse with you." She stole a quick glance in my direction. "Alone."

"We can do that right now, can't we?"

Athena's cheeks turned pink as she balled her fists. "There

is…much I wish to see of this world, should you allow it. And if we are to fight side by side, I hope to know you better, as well. So much cannot be accomplished by speaking solely within the confines of a single room." She flicked her head up with this last point, punctuating her words with a defiant air.

To be fair, since Lily and I were at school during most of the day and always walked home together, there really hadn't been a lot of time to talk one-on-one (outside of our daily training sessions), or show her around the area.

"So…like a date?"

"N-n-not at all!" Athena narrowed her eyes on me as her blush deepened. "The bond shared between comrades should never be mistaken for that of romantic entanglement! I simply hope to become more knowledgeable of this transitory home, and to further strengthen our ties outside the battlefiel– "

"I'm kidding - kidding," I said, trying to suppress a smile as I waved off her concerns. "I'd been thinking I should show you more of the city already. Was there anywhere specific you wanted to go?"

"The destination is unimportant, so long as it should suffice in your eyes…" she mumbled, dropping her gaze to the floor.

"Then…how about we go somewhere tomorrow afternoon? I'm sure I'll think of a place by then, and I can let Lily know in advance."

Athena gave a curt nod. "Very well. For sake of maintaining your energy, we shall postpone our training for one day."

I wasn't sure which was more shocking – Athena acting so embarrassed, or actually cancelling training for a day. At least I could rest easy –

"Of course, in order to keep pace, our efforts must be redoubled during the next session."

Ah. There it was.

"Right, well – " My muscles ached at the mere thought. "I'm looking forward to tomorrow. I think it'll be fun."

"Yes, agreed." Athena finally seemed to relax, looking me in the eye for the first time since entering the room. "Though if you have no further need of me, I shall take my leave."

"Mhm, I'll see you tonight."

At this point I had given up hope that either girl would ever use one of the spare beds in the house.

Still, as Athena closed the door and went back downstairs, a little bit of excitement started to rile inside as I thought about finally getting to know her better. Given how unexpectedly she had bustled into my life, I think we still both saw each other as relative strangers. despite whatever budding friendship had begun to develop. Even though I had picked up bits of info about where she came from and what her past life was like, it was difficult to get to know her on a deeper level without more organic opportunities for conversation and experience. I hoped this might be my chance to change that.

Pulling out a tourist brochure I had tucked away in a drawer (the school had been giving them out in the lead-up to the festival, suggesting students hand them out to friends and family outside the area), I scanned over a list of popular attractions nearby. Despite her preoccupation with "glory" and fighting, Athena seemed to be pretty bookish in her downtime – when she wasn't tending to the garden, I'd usually find her completely invested in something taken off my bookshelf, sitting quietly at her usual spot in the living room. I had amassed a small collection of historical literature over the past few years, ranging from in-depth discussions of revolutions to broader depictions of the history of nations, so I was more than happy to let her indulge in what little I had to offer.

"Then maybe…there."

I ran my finger across the colorful page and stopped on a large square near the middle of the city. A general museum was situated there, which seemed as good a place as any to start if Athena really wanted to learn more about the human world. Satisfied, I folded up the brochure and returned to my notes, trying to absorb as much as I could while my mind continued to wander back to the next day's outing.

* * *

"You sure you'll be ok on your own?" I asked as Lily pushed me and Athena out the door.

"Yes, yes," she said with a weary smile. "Promise I can take care of myself for a few hours. Now go, go, before it starts getting too late."

"Lily, I – " Athena planted her feet in the doorway, hesitant. "I do not mean to impose upon you, however – "

"Really, it's ok." She shook her head wistfully, as if talking to a child. "Like I said, it's not fair if Yuu spends all his time with me alone. I want you to get to know him, too."

"Yes, but you see – I have no intention of overstepping my bounds, and so – "

"Go, go!" Lily laughed to herself and pushed Athena forward once more, easing the door shut behind her. "You'll be late if you don't get going now, so have fun and be safe."

She paused and added quietly: "Please."

"Yes, of cou– " Athena tried to say as Lily locked the door, leaving us next to an empty road lined by dark streetlights in the middle of what was an otherwise quintessential peaceful, "normal" neighborhood.

I glanced at Athena and shrugged. "Shall we?"

With a quick nod she strode forward, forcing me to spring a few steps to catch up. While it took some doing to convince her not to bring along her armor and weapon (Lily, for her part, was instrumental in explaining why keeping a low profile was most convenient for going out), I was happy to see that Athena, at least in street clothes, passed well for an ordinary human.

An admittedly very tall, very, very pretty human - but a human nonetheless.

Even in just a simple pair of jeans and white sweater, her presence was almost overwhelming. Whereas Lily's innocent and earnest nature shone through in the way she attacked each experience with excitement and vigor, Athena was like a statue – beautiful and noble, yet all too often cold and distant. While I had seen cracks in this visage a number of times, she usually carried with her an air of confidence that wasn't necessarily haughty, but made it difficult for someone to feel like they were on the same level as her. It wouldn't be a bold claim to suggest that she was at the top in terms of looks, intelligence, and strength, but I figured it had to be lonely up there by yourself.

Didn't it?

Athena was never particularly unfriendly toward me (that first night we spent together more or less killed any fears that she really disliked me), but I still felt like I was having difficulty connecting with her beyond superficial knowledge of our respective lives. We spent every morning in the yard training, and likewise I would see her every evening at home, but it always felt like she was trying to keep some kind of distance between us. It was possible that I had just gotten too used to how open Lily was about everything, and so found it more difficult to talk with Athena by contrast. Still, whatever the reason, I hoped today would give me the chance to bridge the gap between us, if only a little.

"Is something the matter?"

Athena looked at me with a puzzled expression, as I realized in an instant that I had been staring at her in complete silence.

"Oh, no, uh – " I whipped my head to the side, suddenly enthralled by the bare bushes we were passing by. "I was just, um…wondering if you could tell me more about where you came from."

Athena brought a finger to her lips and pondered my question, which gave me a chance to recover and *actually* appreciate the scenery for a bit. Since we were walking in the opposite direction of the usual route I took to get to the city, we ended up passing through a number of other neighborhoods I rarely had the chance to see otherwise. Given that my house stood on the outskirts of our own block, any time I went out I would have to venture some way through the suburbs.

Despite how cramped it could be in places, the area was lush with variety – tiny wooden homes pressed up against tall stone facades, houses seeming to stretch and squeeze in every direction, and any way you looked offered an entirely new style. From what I understood, this this was all an indirect result of the city's expansion – my parents had told me a number of years ago that the neighborhood our house was in started small, but when the surrounding districts started growing unexpectedly, more and more houses had to be built, often without much regard to how well they fit (aesthetically or otherwise) with the other buildings. In the end, our own home, meant to blend in and match with those around it, stood out even more for how comparatively plain it was.

As I continued to mull over the nuances of architectural aesthetics, Athena tilted her head towards the sky and spoke up again. "I fear I may not be able to relate my experiences in a way that would be comprehensible for a mortal."

"I've...seen some pretty weird stuff already. You might be surprised."

She glanced at me and smiled. "Perhaps so. As you may recall, I hail from what is known as the realm of heroes. It is a land where the most valiant of warriors are born, their skills honed and refined through trial and task. It is a world where an individual's worth is determined solely by the strength of their deeds. The terrain itself is ever-expansive, with crimson-capped mountains formed by the hands of giants caught only by the mauve roiling skies, perpetually stirred by the hands of gods. Each morning a blazing dawn scorches the treetops in an auburn cape, and each evening countless stars stream past in a restless pursuit of some unknown destination."

"That sounds incredible, though I - " I gave a sheepish laugh. "I don't think there's anything that can compare around here. Just a lot of tall of buildings and trees."

"Then perhaps..."

"Hm?"

"My apologies, pay it no mind." Athena shook her head. "Would you still like to know more?"

"Yeah, of course. I want to learn as much about you as I can."

"Very well."

It might've been my imagination, but I could've sworn I saw her smile widen just a little.

"As you might expect, such perfect grace cannot long exist unsoiled. Since the earliest records, a plague of monstrous entities, hailing from worlds both near and far to my own, have roamed the terrain. That is why the spirits of my realm – the order I was raised in – pledge themselves to the blade. What thin vestiges of safety remain must be ardently protected."

"You mean that sisterhood you were talking about before?"

"The very one. The Order of Arta maintains fortresses across the realm, with the hopes of one day eradicating the threats present in our world. To fact, the complex I called home served as a forward bastion in these efforts, though, despite my sisters' best efforts, we have found little success in quelling such blight. Still, we train and fight each and every day, ever-hopeful that we may expand the boundaries of civilization and bring prosperity back to a world overrun."

Even though I couldn't pin down exactly what it was, something seemed to change when Athena started talking about the monsters in her world. She spoke coldly and plainly, with none of the passion that normally shone clear in her voice.

"Did you not like it there? I mean, I can't imagine having to fight for survival all the time is the best way to live."

She closed her eyes and shook her head slowly. "No, to the contrary – it was an honor to be brought to that realm. Walking the marble halls, passing by heroes of legend immortalized in silver, and those pedestals yet awaiting to be adorned, one could not help but be overtaken with humility and awe. As our instructors would remind us: 'From nothing we are born, to nothing we will return.' Regardless of one's birthright, each individual is afforded an equal chance to lay stake their claim for glory."

"Then…did you have to fight a lot while yourself while you were there?"

Although I had only seen her matched up against myself

and two other humans, the way Athena so naturally wielded her sword during practice – despite its immense size, she easily used it with one hand – seemed to indicate her prior experience.

"Yes, battle was a regular occurrence for all those who were part of the Order. We would foray into the thickest forests and deepest valleys in hopes of clearing a path for further encampments. Though I must confess that, when I was suddenly thrust into your world, I was still not long from my own training."

As I prepared to ask more about her daily life in the hero realm, Athena offered a question of her own.

"Tell me – do you believe I revel in battle?"

Her tone was completely neutral, so it was difficult to figure out what her true intentions were, or how I should answer. Seeing nothing else to go on, I simply had to be honest.

"I'm not really sure. I mean, I would say fighting is important to you, but I don't think that's what makes you who you are."

"Oh?" Athena stopped and turned to face me. "How do you mean?"

"Well, y'know – as far as I can tell, you're not lacking in strength or ability, and I think you see fighting as a way to protect the things that're important to you. But I wouldn't say you enjoy fighting just for the sake of it. It's more like...your own way of showing you care."

Athena nodded to herself and continued walking. "I do not crave conflict, nor do I desire bloodshed. However, what I am, and who I am, may not be so easily disentangled as you suggest..."

As she trailed off, gaze fixed ahead toward some indiscernible entity on the horizon, I figured it was best to switch topics and not press the issue any further.

"Outside of that, was there anything you liked to do with your free time?"

We were approaching the city limits, but there was still time for a little more casual conversation.

"Free time?"

"Yeah, like hobbies and stuff. When you didn't have to go fight or train or anything."

"Ah, those recesses from battle and study. I suppose I spent most of my spare hours reading. The library afforded to us was immense, and held the knowledge of scholars spanning both time and realms. During those brief periods I was not called to action, I would borrow tomes of every sort to scour through in seclusion, away from the clatter of others."

"Huh, that almost sounds like me in a way."

"Oh?" Athena smiled softly to herself, a curious glint in her eyes.

"I don't really like going out that much, so I usually spend my spare time hidden away in my room with a book. I tend to like history the most, since they're like real world adventures, though – I guess you, uh, probably already knew that."

"While it is true few selections can match that of the Order's, I still must thank you for allowing me to partake in what you have accumulated. The perception of humans can be just as foreign to a spirit as the worlds of spirits are to a mortal."

"Huh, I…never really thought about it that way."

"You can hardly be faulted. The limited lives of mortals naturally lead them to understand past events in a vastly different way than those whose existence are effectively endless. And yet – there remains a shared history all the same."

"Yeah, that's what got me interested in the first place." I

leaned up against Athena to avoid getting in the way of a man in a suit running down the street, briefcase in one hand and a crumpled piece of paper in the other. "Watching all these things happen around me, I always wanted to know more. I never thought I could do anything worthwhile myself, so I settled for reading about the people who had made a name for themselves, who were important enough to be remembered. Although, since meeting you and Lily, maybe I've gotten more than I bargained for."

I shook my head and laughed in resignation.

"I dunno, saying it out loud like that makes me realize how dumb it all sounds."

"No!" Athena placed a hand on my shoulder and pulled me aside, out of the way of oncoming foot traffic. "Do not say such things. The passions you maintain, the things you value – you must hold to them dearly and not let go, come whatever may. They will be your guiding light, and your drive to continue." As she continued to stare at me with a fixed intensity, her expression softened. "It ails me to hear you discount such things so easily."

"Alright, I won't, I won't," I said with a half-smile. "Thank you. It's…nice to hear someone say that."

Satisfied, Athena released me and allowed us to continue on our way, reaching our destination only a few blocks later. From what I was able to look up, the museum was host to a somewhat eclectic collection of art and artifacts, with a focus on how societies have formed and developed over time. Given that there was no one specific region or country as the basis, however, there wasn't a lot of consistency in what was on display. Still, this seemed like the kind of place that would interest her, and might give her a good foundation for understanding this world on her own terms.

As we stepped up to the entrance, I couldn't help but take note of the fact that it was a little less grand than what one might expect when hearing the word "museum". The outside was made of plain brick, with only a humble bronze plate to the left of the door to indicate the building's purpose:

"Empire City Museum of Human Civilization"

My first thought was that the name was a little redundant, given there were no other civilizations than those of the human variety, though I quickly remembered that recent events had quite handily shattered this assumption. Putting aside this realization, I pushed open the sturdy wooden door as Athena followed me inside.

"What manner of place is this?" she asked in a voice mixed with excitement and confusion.

The lobby was sparsely furnished, with worn reds and muted greens adorning the carpet and walls and a single worn bench placed off in a corner. A wide desk stood in the center, books and papers of every size and color spread across it. The only other person present was a single attendant wearing a crisp jacket and unassuming gold pin, who greeted us quickly and politely when we entered, then returned to what I assumed was the museum's archives through a door in the back, leaving the two of us alone.

"This is a museum – it's sort of like a library, but without the books."

"Then what purpose does it serve?"

"Um, maybe that wasn't the best way to describe it." I gave an awkward laugh as Athena continued to look at me curiously. "I meant that there's a lot you can learn here, like at the library. That's why I thought you might like it. Just instead of books, there's these displays you can look at and learn about. Since this one is all about human development, I thought it might help you get acquainted with this world."

Athena turned her head away in a huff. "Would you assume that I know so little about your kind and this realm?"

"No, no, I didn't mean it like that! I just – I thought you might want to learn about the history of this world, too."

"You needn't be so sensitive, I merely tease," Athena said with a pitying smile. "Though it is true that I may be more knowledgeable of this world than spirits of other realms."

"Wait, so you learned about humans even in your world?"

"Yes, humanity remained a perpetual source of fascination for my sisters and, should our literary collection be proof of anything, at least of passing interest for scholars. However, I learned largely through more…practical means."

"Practical?"

Athena nodded, taking a seat on the bench and gesturing for me join her. "As you may recall, the spirits from each realm share varying levels of familiarity with humans. Spirits such as I and my sisters regularly communed with mortals, and, through our repeated tenure here, learned much of this world. Should any feat of bravery or battle be needed, we were called upon to provide guidance and strength."

"I think I understand," I said slowly, working over what Athena said. "So kind of like what I have with you and Lily, right?"

"Not quite. The contract forged between you and I is of a stronger nature than those prayers regularly conducted by mortals. Should a human request the aid of a spirit, and should they offer sufficient compensation, some manner of assistance will be given, per said spirit's specialty. Forging a contract, however – " Athena crossed her legs, pausing to search for the right words. "Is something of an entirely different magnitude. It is a bond forged within a mortal's very soul."

"And…you still want me to do that with any spirits that show up around here, right?"

"I understand it is a sizable request, but its importance cannot be overstated. If you are able to do so, their presence will be stabilized, thus preventing the further intrusion of wayward spirits and creatures into this realm." Athena beamed with an understated joy. "You have the potential to save an untold number of lives, and to become the protector of this town – nay, perhaps even this world. You should take pride in your position."

"I…I'll do my best," I murmured, trying to force a smile in return. "But there's actually something else I wanted to ask you about."

"Oh?"

I hesitated, unsure if I *really* wanted to hear the answer to this question. "When we first met, Lily said that for a human to make a contract with a spirit, they have to give up a part of their soul."

Athena nodded along. "That is correct."

"Well…" Given her blasé response, I wasn't sure if she already knew what was coming next. "She also said that if I lose enough of my soul, I'll die. Or rather, cease to exist."

"I suppose that would be the natural result."

I felt my heart stop.

Was that it? Did she really not care about me at all? Had I been too quick to trust her, and assumed she wouldn't try to hurt me? Maybe this was just how spirits viewed humans – tools to be used and discarded. And if that was the case, then didn't I *need* to break this contract somehow? I didn't want to die like that, I didn't –

"Yuu?" Athena placed a soft hand against my forehead. "You've grown ghastly pale. Is something the matter?"

"Do you really not care if I disappear?" I said quietly.

"What do you mean?"

"You just said that would happen if I keep making contracts. And…and isn't that what you want?"

Athena stared at me for a few seconds, before letting out a suppressed giggle.

"W-what's so funny?"

"Nothing, nothing at all – I was simply unaware that such worries clouded your mind."

I felt a comfortable warmth as Athena lightly took my hand in hers.

"Yes, it is true that when a being loses their soul – be they mortal or monster – they enter a state between realms, neither fully alive nor deceased. However, human souls are unique, as they are not limited in their capacity to bond to others. The stronger this grows –" She took one of my fingers and poked it against my chest. "The more bountiful your soul will become, as well. So please, fear not – I chose you not for any innate prowess or ability, but rather the selfless magnanimity you demonstrated in protecting those around you. So long as these intentions stay true, your soul will only strengthen – not diminish – as you commune with additional spirits."

"Then…I'll be ok?"

"I promised you and your paramour that I would always protect you, did I not? I am not so callous as to place you in harm's way for my own ends, rest assured."

"Right, you're…you're right. Thank you."

I felt a pang of guilt for doubting Athena so easily. She could be harsh at times, and maybe a little difficult to understand, but she really wasn't the type to take advantage of someone else. It wasn't fair of me to distrust her like that.

"Anyway, I think I've kept us side-tracked long enough," I said, hopping to my feet. "Why don't we check out the rest of the museum?"

Athena followed close behind as we ventured into the first exhibit, where crude stone tools were strewn about next to faux animal pelts and bits of copper that might've once adorned some hunter's knife, or an aspiring decadent's necklace. The glass cases that housed these items each had a small placard describing their origins and use.

One in particular stuck out to me – a thin, chipped piece of bark with faded and smudged markings scattered across its face. From what the accompanying plate said, this was thought to be an early attempt at writing, though the lack of any additional records made it impossible to know what was actually trying to be conveyed.

"Has something caught your attention?" Athena asked, peering over my shoulder.

"Oh, no, it's just – " I glanced back at the makeshift tablet – lifeless, worn, silent. "I can't help but wonder why people do the things they do."

She stepped away, heading towards the next room. "Elaborate."

"Well…when humans first started writing things down, why did they do it? No one can understand them now, so did it even mean anything in the first place? And will the same thing happen to me? I – "

I sighed and stepped up to the tattered pages of some

manuscript describing a medical treatment that, given the variety of poisonous ingredients suggested, I had to assume was more fatal than helpful.

"I know I shouldn't be bringing up something so heavy out of the blue. I guess with so much changing lately, I've had a lot on my mind."

"Not at all – if there is anything to human nature, it is the indelible curiosity that stokes one to question why. I find nothing strange about that."

We passed by a display of an armored knight frozen in time, forever ready to plunge his spear into his robed adversary, splayed and helpless on the ground.

"Then what do you think?"

"All things pass on in their due course, that is true. The greatest of empires have succumbed to decay all the same as the most mundane of lives. However – "

Athena stopped in front of a large painting, which nearly spread from floor to ceiling.

"Do you know the story of this piece?"

The painting depicted a wizened old man, tufts of grey hair spouting out of a red and gold cap, holding out a thin paintbrush in a trembling hand, poised to bring life to an empty canvas. His surroundings were drab, with a collapsed wooden table and turned over chair as the only accompanying furniture. A dirt floor and dark corners juxtaposed against the sunny green hillside just visible through a small, circular window to the side.

"Not really, but it looks pretty straight-forward. It's an old man painting – maybe a self-portrait?"

"Yes, that is the substance of what is represented, though, as I am sure you are aware, there is much more to meaning than what is apparent on the surface."

She pointed to the man, so lifelike and detailed that it felt like he could move his hand at any moment.

"The subject of this work is Lorenzo Foretti, a renowned painter of antiquity. As legend tells, he was rarely seen outside his home, wiling away at his canvas from the earliest morning past latest evening. One day, however, a young boy stumbled across his hut and, ever the curious and impetuous child, let himself in to see who might be home."

"And I'm guessing Lorenzo was there, painting?" I said with a half-grin.

Athena rolled her eyes, though I could see a hint of her own smile. "Yes, you are correct. The boy saw wondrous works unlike any he had ever laid eyes on cluttering the walls of the shabby abode. He asked the man why he would waste his hours tucked away in a hovel such as this, when outside his door was an endless bounty of even more impressive vistas. Foretti remained silent as the boy argued for all the overwhelming beauty that could not be captured in a mere portrait, and only appreciated through one's experiences."

"So what'd Lorenzo say?"

"Foretti placed down his brush and removed the canvas from the easel, placing the finished piece next to all the others he had accumulated. He then turned to the boy, and spoke plainly: 'If I do not do this, then who will?'"

Athena paused, allowing me a moment of reflection.

"Do you see now? At times, action need only validate itself."

"Yeah – " I continued to inspect the painting, entranced by its hidden story. "Just doing something for the sake of doing it is enough?"

"I believe that is the moral presented. It is a distinctly human convention, though a fascinating one none–"

Athena cut herself off, her attention fixed behind me.

"Did something hap–"

"Sh."

She held a finger to her lips and stepped in front of me. I strained to pick up on what she was listening for even as the museum was near-silent, save for the far-off shuffling of papers and occasional footsteps.

"Hey, is everything ok? You're acting kind of w–"

"Listen."

She leaned down and held her arm out in front of me, keeping me back. Again, I tried to focus all my attention on listening for whatever might be making her so jumpy, but nothing came. Until –

rrrrrrr

A low rumbling, almost like a growl, drifted toward us from a nearby corner of the room. The museum must not've been renovated in some time, as the lighting for each area was incredibly dim, making it difficult to see beyond what was on display in the exhibits themselves. I bent down to try to see what might be the source of this strange noise, but anything a few feet past the scant light fixtures remained obfuscated by darkness.

"Maybe it's something outside – "

My voice failed as, out of the corner of my eye, I saw three figures step out of the shadows.

11

"Athena?"

Three creatures crept forward, bearing the overall shape of a wolf, but with formless bodies black enough to stand out against the shadows they came out of, lacking any discernable fur or joints. The only other color present on their being was the vibrant, near-luminous red of their eyes, now honed on the two of us.

"*Athena?*" I repeated.

My legs were rooted to the ground and my arms hung limp at my side, as if my body understood on some visceral level that these creatures were unnatural, belonging to neither this world nor any I would ever wish to conceive of.

"You know what must be done." Athena spoke quietly, never taking her eyes off the pulsating figures in front of us.

"You don't mean - "

The single look she shot in my direction was all the confirmation I needed.

"O-ok."

There was no use in arguing. This was what I had been training for, after all.

I took a deep breath and tried to clear my mind. I couldn't let my fear get the best of me. I may have been useless before, but now – now I had the means to protect us. As I felt a faint heat rise within my chest, I placed my hand against it, and –

Nothing.

I pushed harder.

Still nothing.

I pressed my hand with all my might, but flesh and bone still blocked the way. The wolf-like creatures continued their steady advance, haunches raised and heads bowed low, the guttural rumbling growing louder with each step they took.

"Is something the matter?"

"No, I – "

I slammed my fist into my chest, trying to replicate what I had done a hundred times before in practice.

"Just a – "

I pushed and pressed and dug, to no avail.

"Little trouble – "

Before Athena could respond, the creature at the front of the pack rushed forward, lunging straight at me. I winced and turned to the side, ready to brace against its attack, when it suddenly went tumbling, landing on the ground in a crumpled heap. With one blindingly fast move, Athena had drove her fist into the creature's maw, swatting it away with incredible strength.

"I will hold them off long as I am able, though I advise you to hasten your efforts."

"I...I will."

I took another deep breath, felt the warmth emanating from within rise up once more, and prepared to reach for my blade, when the two remaining beasts attacked together. Athena was able to grab one by the scruff of its neck and toss it away, though this left the other an opening to come from behind.

Without thinking, I jumped in front of her, bringing my arms across my chest. I saw the creature's teeth tear into my arm, but, whether due to adrenalin or Lily's influence, felt comparatively little pain. I threw my arm out and tried to shake free from its grip, though the weight of the monster was enough to pull me to the ground, swiftly repositioning as it snapped furiously at my neck, while I struggled to hold it back.

In one last act of desperation, I slipped a hand into my chest, and – miraculously – feflt a burst of heat as I grabbed onto the rusty and chipped blade Athena had bestowed on me. I hastily tore it out, turning the hilt at the last moment and driving it through the monster's belly, the blade slipping through with minimal effort. The creature at last relented, as a moment later its body crumbled apart and faded into nothingness.

I scrambled to my feet as the first wolf limped back in to view, its killing intent unmitigated despite its injured state. Going on pure instinct alone, I ran toward it, startling the monster as I brought my sword down onto its neck, easily dispelling whatever force had been keeping its vague form intact.

However, as I turned around to face the last creature, an enraged snarl came just before a pair of thick claws dug deep into my back, scraping down my skin as it fought to hold on. I was forced back down to my knees, and might've collapsed once more had Athena not grabbed the creature by its upper jaw and tore it away.

Despite the ease with which I was able to slay the first two creatures, I felt my strength rapidly depleting, as I could now barely able to stagger to my feet. Nevertheless, I forced myself to hobble onward, trying to get to the monster before it could recover, when Athena brought her arm under mine and, holding my hand in hers, plunged the sword into the wolf's side, leaving only a few dusty ashes as any proof of its existence.

"You…think that's all of them?" I panted, dropping to the floor. Even though the fight couldn't have lasted more than a minute or two, I felt completely exhausted, my head spinning and muscles weak.

"It would seem so," Athena said as she knelt down beside me and gingerly took my arm in her hands, looking it over carefully. "Though I am glad to see you've taken our lessons to heart – "

She pulled on the blood-soaked sleeve, causing me to wince. Whatever pain I was able to ignore before had now caught back up to me.

"I see there is still much left to teach you."

"Like?" I said with a wry smile.

"How to dodge, for one – " She tugged on the sleeve again, pulling out the pieces of cloth that had been driven into the gashes. "Try to move your fingers now."

I rolled my fingers into and out of a fist, sending a fresh wave of pain through my arm. I gritted my teeth and tried to bear with it, not wanting to come across as even more pathetic than I knew I really was.

"Good. It would appear there was no lasting injury. Come – " She stood back up and wrapped her arm around my body. "We should return home before these wounds fester."

"Y-yeah, thanks."

I gladly leaned on her support as we started to make our way out of the museum.

"So what – " I looked around as we entered the next exhibit room, adjacent to the lobby. Fortunately the museum was still just as vacant as when we first arrived. "What were those things back there?"

"Those creatures?" Athena adjusted her arm, hoisting me up higher. "I must profess I have never come across a being of that kind myself - and yet they have been dispatched all the same, so we needn't dwell upon it a moment longer."

"Yeah, but – " I sighed and shuffled forward with her. "Maybe you're right."

As we reached the front entrance, Athena paused.

"Before we disembark - "

"Huh?"

"I must chide you for your recklessness – " She looked down at me and smiled, placing her other arm over my shoulder. "And commend you for your bravery. Though it was foolish to throw yourself in harm's way for my sake, it would be unjust to not thank you for it."

I felt my cheeks burning as she slowly pulled me closer, letting my head rest against her. I was no stranger to Athena's sporadic displays of affection, but something in the way she held me now felt different from before – less like a mentor and student, and almost more like two lov–

"Ah. It's you again."

This line of thinking was abruptly interrupted by the door being thrown open, as a tall, thin man in a freshly-pressed suit stood before us.

Rick sounded less surprised than disappointed, as Athena tightened her hold on me.

"Yuu?" Athena said in a low voice, tightening her hold on me. "Who is this man?"

"A, uh – "

"A friend of his," Rick said with what might charitably be described as a "smile". He held out his hand, which Athena carefully shook, though she still kept one arm wrapped around my head.

Rick tried to peek behind Athena, who, given her height and the size of the doorway, was blocking most of the entrance. "Seems like trouble has a way of following you around, huh?"

"Oh, you know how it is…" I muttered.

"Well, no need for formalities this time around." Rick stretched his arms in the air and glanced behind him, where a number of familiarly innocuous cars were parked. "I'm sure you already know why I'm here, so why don't you just give me the run down on what happened and I'll let you be on your way."

I didn't see any reason to try to lie about it, so I tried my best to describe the shadowy wolf-creatures that had suddenly appeared inside the museum, conveniently leaving out anything related to Athena's true nature, and suggesting that the creatures disappeared into some other part of the museum after losing interest in us.

"Strange things, huh? To be honest, I've never heard of something like that showing up either, let alone in a place like this. But then again, given how little we know about the other realms, maybe that shouldn't come as a surprise."

I couldn't be certain, but I got the feeling this was Rick's attempt to open up to me.

"Anyway, thanks for your help. We'll handle things from here on out, so you two be safe heading home."

"Will do."

As Athena pulled me forward and brushed past Rick, I noticed her watching him closely, his own interest piqued in return. It wasn't until we were a few blocks away, and well out of earshot, that she spoke up again.

"That man…"

"Rick?"

She nodded, still holding me close. "I believe he is aware of more than he lets on."

"How do you think?"

For whatever reason I got a similarly weird vibe from Rick, so I was keen on getting an honest second opinion.

"His awareness of the other worlds alone is nothing if not suspect. It is exceptionally rare for modern humans to have any conception that such things exist beyond the realms of myth and legends."

"He said he works for some government agency that regularly deals with this sort of thing, so maybe it's just all routine to him?"

"Perhaps…" Athena went quiet for a moment, then shook her head. "No, I know too little of this man to judge him fairly. Though I sense no ill will from him, I believe prudence is the best course in any further dealings you may have with him."

"Yeah, you're probably right."

The rest of the walk home took place mostly in comfortable silence, giving me time to reflect on the day's events.

This was my second time facing off against an otherworldly creature and, while the results were admittedly better than when I tried to take on the minotaur, I still almost let someone get hurt because of my own carelessness. I knew it was silly to compare myself to a spirit that had been training for this kind of thing for what might've been centuries, but I couldn't so easily brush off the responsibility I'd now chosen to inherit (if only temporarily). Whether I was strong enough or not didn't matter – I promised to take care of Athena and Lily, and I would have to find a way to do that, whatever it took.

Beyond that, I had to agree with Athena's assessment of Rick

– I didn't think he was necessarily a bad guy, but I also couldn't shake the feeling that there was more going on than he was letting on. Even if he appeared honest enough, and what he was doing (working to protect the public from otherworldly creatures and all) was a noble enough pursuit, I still felt uneasy around him. Until I figured out why, I'd have a hard time placing any real trust in him.

* * *

By the time we reached the house, the sun had already set, the glow of porchlights and litted windows illuminating our way alongside the frosty street lamps. We had decided to skip going out to eat, considering the sorry state I was in, and the fact that I was still feeling pretty woozy from before. As I stumbled through the front door, I felt a wave of relief wash over, happily assured that the day's excitement was over with.

At least until I saw what was waiting for me inside.

"Yuu! You're home!"

Lily was standing in the middle of the kitchen, clad in nothing more than a simple kitchen apron and holding a ladle to her chest.

"Uh, Lily, what are you doing?"

I feared I already knew the answer, but I had to ask anyway.

Lily clasped her hands together, fidgeting nervously. "I know you've been working really hard lately and you seemed really stressed, so I wanted to give you a surprise for when you came home."

"I...definitely am surprised," I murmured to myself.

"I asked Himeo what I should do, since she helped me with this kind of thing before, and she said if I put something like this on it would make you happy."

She glanced up, her innocent gaze sending my heart rate skyrocketing.

"Did it?"

"Yes, it's really – I mean, it's, um…"

Words failed me as I looked upon the sight set before me.

Given our sleeping arrangements, I was no stranger to the contours of Lily's body, and she was always forthcoming when it came to physical affection. However, this stood in a league entirely of its own – the innocent and demure appearance, the sensual nakedness hiding just beneath, and the indirect aggressiveness of such an outfit were almost too much to bear.

Still, no matter how openly she presented herself, I had to respect the fact that, deep down, Lily didn't necessarily understand what she was doing. She had never tried to initiate any kind of sexual intimacy, and I always had to assume she was just unaware of the tertiary effects this kind of thing had on me.

Even it was difficult at times to hold my own desires back, I had to be strong. She meant much more to me than just her body, and when the time came that we were ready to take the next step – when she fully understood what sharing ourselves in such a way truly meant – I was sure it'd be worth the wait.

So for now –

"You look amazing. You…really, really do. But – "

I could feel Athena's stare burning into the back of my head.

"We, um, didn't have a chance to eat, so why don't I cook something up for us?"

It was all I could think of to divert attention away from Lily's unique choice of attire.

"No, no, that's my job today!"

Lily pouted and leaned forward, forcing me to find immense interest in the clock affixed on the wall behind her in order to avoid catching an unintentional eyeful. I calmly reminded myself that she didn't realize the implications of what she was doing, and surely had no other interest than trying to make me smile. She was just being her sweet, silly self, nothing more.

Totally…completely…absolutely.

"But you still don't know how to cook, r…right?"

Another bout of lightheadedness, though I shook it off as nothing more than fatigue.

"Maybe not a lot, but it can't be that hard, right? You just put some food together and then…you…" Lily took a step forward, looking at me with concern. "Yuu? Is something wrong?"

"Huh? Me? No, I – "

My vision started to blur as my body grew heavy.

"I-I'm fine, really. I might just need…to…lie – "

That was the last thing I remember before blacking out.

12

"…tect…m."

"I…ed…en…eed…op."

As I started to come to, I overheard Lily and Athena's muffled voices nearby. Although every aching muscle in my body was telling me to close my eyes and go back to sleep, I felt I should get up and at least tell them I was ok. And so, pulling together my willpower, I rolled on to my side and tried to push myself up -

Immediately sending a tearing pain through my arm and forcing me to cry out.

Within the next moment Lily had thrown open the door, Athena hovering right behind her.

"Yuu! Are you ok? Are you awake now? What hurts?"

Before I could say anything, Lily had rushed to the side of the bed and was carefully scrutinizing my arm, which I now realized was bandaged over. As I shifted to try to sit up, I felt a tightness on my back that seemed to indicate the same had been done to the injuries there too.

"I'm – I'm fine, really," I said with a weak smile. Even though a dull pain continued to pulsate throughout my body, I didn't want to give Lily any more cause to worry. "I heard you and Athena talking out in the hallway - is everything ok?"

Lily gently pushed me back down on to the bed, giving a pitying look as she ran her fingers through my hair. "Yes, everything's fine. It will be fine."

"That's good, I didn't mean to sc– "

"I don't think Athena should stay with us any longer."

"Wait, what?" I tried to lurch forward, but Lily, anticipating this, kept her hand on my shoulder, holding me back.

"She promised me she would protect you. She said she wouldn't let anything happen to you. And yet you came home like this…" Lily ran her hand across my arm, where dark crimson splotches stained the otherwise pristine wrap. "She lied to me. She lied to us. We don't need someone like that anymore."

"Lily, I – "

Her eye lacked the usual care and gentleness I'd come to expect. In its place was neither anger, nor sadness, nor even fear; rather, they were empty. Devoid of any emotion or feeling, a hollow black that seemed to only look through me.

"I want you to listen to me very carefully." I said, placing an unsteady hand on her cheek. "I don't know what Athena told you, but what happened earlier was my fault, and mine alone. The only reason I got hurt in the first place was due to my own frailty and inexperience. She did everything she could to protect me, and it would've been a lot worse without her. So if you need to blame anyone, blame me."

I moved my other hand over hers, but she only shook her head slowly.

"No…no, no. If she hadn't shown up, if she hadn't insisted on you helping her, if she hadn't put these crazy ideas in your head, you wouldn't have gotten hurt." Lily leaned close, pressing her forehead against mine. "We don't need anyone else, ok? Just you and me. Like it should be. Like it always should've been. Like it needs to be – "

"I think that's enough."

Athena's shadow loomed over the two of us, though Lily didn't so much as glance back at her.

"You don't need to meddle in our life anymore." She rested her head on my shoulder, a joyless smile on her lips. "Don't you think you've already caused him enough trouble as it is? He doesn't need you, he doesn't want you, and you don't even belong here, so you can just go."

"No, that's not - "

In one motion Athena grabbed Lily by the collar (she must've changed into pajamas sometime while I was out cold) and pulled her to her feet.

"I. Told. You." Athena moved to the bed and pulled my shirt up, exposing the pattern etched into my chest. "Should I even want to, I would be unable. So long as there is a contract between mortal and spirit, neither can stray far from the other. Be it by force or persuasion, the two will always come to be reunited."

"Then end the contract."

"You know – "

"I won't say it again." Lily spoke with a cold conviction I had only heard from her once before. "Leave. Now."

Athena crossed her arms, staring down at Lily. "And what right have you to make such demands?"

"I'm his girlfriend." She dropped her hand to her side and slowly moved it back. "But what are you? Some lost little girl? Some interloper trying to break us apart? I can't tell if you're evil or just stupid, but either way – "

"LILY, NO!"

Mustering what little energy I had left, I threw myself off the bed and grabbed Lily's arm, just as the scythe materialized in her hands. I slumped to the ground, holding my arms tight around her wrist.

"I...don't want...you...to fight..."

My heart was racing and my muscles burning, but I couldn't let go. Not until she was back to normal.

"You have to...have to listen to me..."

"Yuu?" Lily turned her head, confused. "What – did I – "

Glancing at the weapon in her hand, she sunk to her knees as it returned to its original state, fluttering to the ground in a tangled heap.

"I...I did it again..." she said blankly. "Why...I..."

I pulled myself up and rested against her back, wrapping my arms around her shoulders. "It's – it's ok now. That's...not you. Whatever it is, that's not you."

Tears streamed down Lily's cheek as she placed her hand over mine. "It's...not?"

"No, and I believe you know better." Athena knelt down and wiped Lily's cheek, smiling softly. "Some say tempers only flare when one has something truly worth protecting. And yet I would loathe to see that define you."

"You...how can you be so nice to me? After...after what I said...what I did...I..." Lily tried to choke back the flow of tears, her voice barely above a whisper.

"All is forgiven. Now come – we should return Yuu to his bed."

Without waiting for a response, Athena cradled me in her arms and gently lowered me back onto the bed.

"If you would allow, may I continue my explanation?"

Lily gave a small nod, remaining on the floor.

"And you?" Athena looked to me now. "I am certain you are still fatigued, but there is much I must inform you of. It may wait until another time, though expediency would be preferable."

"No, tell me. Please."

"Very well. Do you recall the creatures we encountered earlier?"

I touched the bandage on my arm, the cuts still raw and sensitive, and winced. "Kinda hard to forget."

"And the minotaur you both subdued?"

"Yep."

Still had the scar to prove it.

"Even, I would posit, my own arrival in this place. Three separate events, yet all tied by the unique nature of their origin. It would seem too miraculous to attribute to mere chance."

"So you're saying they're all linked?"

"In a sense, yes. Though the details remain hazy, it is not unreasonable to suggest that the greater the power you harness within your soul, the more spirits and creatures alike you are destined to attract."

"But wait, aren't we trying to *stop* them from coming into this world?"

Athena shook her head. "You misunderstand. It would take a power far beyond what one mortal is capable of to bring beings from another realm to this world. Whatever is causing their appearance is unrelated to the task set before you. However –
"

She sat down on the edge of the bed and pointed at my chest.

"Those that *do* come to this realm will be drawn to the energy you gather. It is as a moth to flame – most will not themselves understand why they are driven in your direction, only possessing some vague awareness that you are the one they must seek out. Of these, some may be benevolent, and others…less so."

I traced my finger over the pattern on my skin, thinking over what Athena said. "But if that's the case, then the more spirits I bond with, the more things will try to to attack us?"

"That is a very possible outcome, though – " She nodded towards Lily. "There is more to this arrangement than may have first been obvious."

"What do you mean?"

"Mortals cannot typically bring harm upon beings from the other realms. It is only when imbued with spiritual energy that they may even hope to oppose them."

Athena brought one leg up as she leaned back, her gaze fixed on Lily.

"I presume that is also why you fainted earlier. In using your blade, you depleted what little energy was available, and so your body shut down in response."

"But wait, wait, wait – then how come that never happened when I was training? I've used my sword plenty of times and never passed out like that."

"Simply calling forth the weapon uses only a marginal amount of energy. It is only when employed in battle, whether with the intent to kill or protect, that its true power is harnessed."

I thought back to our fight against those wolf-things. It did seem like they went down a little *too* easy for someone who had only been learning to fight for a few weeks. Though if what Athena was saying was true, then that meant –

"Just contracting with more spirits will make me stronger?"

Athena bobbed her head to the side. "In a…sense, yes. The

closer your relation to those you bind with, the greater proportion of spiritual energy you will be able to wield. Of course, capacity and ability are of two different considerations."

I forced myself up, looking Athena directly in the eyes.

"Then I'll keep training. Please - whatever I need to do, whatever it takes, I want to get stronger. If...if it means I can protect you both, I'll do it."

Athena closed her eyes and smiled to herself. "Hmhm. I should have expected no less, after all."

She hopped off the bed and walked over to the doorway, peering back at me before leaving.

"I should fetch you a set of fresh bandages before you sleep. I'll be gone only a moment."

With that, she gently closed the door behind her, the trailing sound of footsteps falling away to a now-silent room. Lily still had her back to me, and I wasn't sure what I should – or even could – say in this situation. I had thought that her and Athena were getting along better, and maybe growing closer, but what happened just now pretty handily dismantled that assumption. Plus, deep down I knew, once again –

It was all my fault.

Despite what I wanted to tell myself, despite all the things that I tried to brush off or ignore, I knew it was true. Lily was always averse to confrontation, and only ever manifested that "other" personality when she thought she needed to protect me. The fact that I was too weak to defend myself, that I let myself get hurt and then didn't even try to tell her about it when I had the chance, laid the blame squarely on my shoulders.

And on top of that, supposed noble intentions aside, I *had* invited another woman (spirit or not) into our home. Me and Lily had only been dating for about a week before I went and did something like that – again, all without talking to her about it first. Hell, I was too weak-willed to even tell Athena not to sleep in the same bed as us. I'd been living with the hope – or maybe delusion – that as long as I didn't "do" anything wrong, things would work themselves out.

But life isn't like that.

I had to take responsibility. I had to act. I had to make things right.

"Lily, can I…" My mouth felt dry as the pent-up guilt I'd been trying to tamp down threatened to burst forth all at once. "Can I talk to you?"

Lily nodded, though she didn't budge from her spot on the floor.

"I…want to apologize. For a lot of things."

No response.

"I can't say I know what you've been going through, and…and I should've been more attentive. I should've asked you what's wrong, should've tried to see things from your perspective."

Again, nothing.

"Maybe it's too late to ask you to forgive me, but I still want to do better. I want to make things right."

With a stifled grunt I managed to push myself out of the bed and shuffle back over to Lily.

"It's my fault things turned out this way. I got caught up in this whole thing with Athena, and never really asked you how you felt about it."

I crouched down next to Lily and slowly wrapped my arms around her once more.

"You can blame me for everything and I'll accept it. But please don't hate Athena. I think – no, I know she really cares about you, even if she has a hard time showing it. So please, let me – "

"That's not it," Lily said in a hushed tone. A part of me was immediately relieved just to hear her normal voice again.

"What isn't?"

Lily placed her hands on my arms, pulling me closer. "I don't hate her. I don't hate you. I couldn't…I never could."

"But, what happened back there – "

"I don't know." Lily shook her head, her voice starting to rise. "I don't know I don't know I don't know! Whenever I see you get hurt, it's like someone else takes over."

She pulled on my arms again, tightening the embrace.

"I don't know why it happens, I don't know who it is, I don't know how to make it stop, I don't – "

She shook her head again, as if trying to cast away the fears haunting her.

"I don't want you to hate me. I don't want you to think I'm a monster. I don't want you to leave because you know I'm not a human, I'm not like you, I'm not normal, I'm not – "

"Shh, shh, it's ok," I said softly, slipping one hand away to pet her hair. "Didn't you just say you'd never hate me? The same is true for me."

"But…but why?" Lily sniffled as tears began to overflow again. "I tried to hide it, I tried to hold it back, but you saw what I'll do. Or…or what she'll do." She hung her head, speaking more to herself than me now. "Sometimes I don't even know which is the real me."

"Then…"

There had to be something I could, something I could say to make things right. But first I had to learn more about this other side of her.

"Can you tell me more about it? Or, uh, her?"

"Honestly, I don't know much either. When she comes out, it's like...like this part of me fades away, and all I can do is watch. I remember some of the things that happen, but it's always fuzzy and scattered."

Lily let go of my arms and hugged her knees to her chest.

"That's what scares me the most. Someday I might hurt you and not even know it."

"No, Lily – "

I slowly turned her around so that we could talk face-to-face. My chest tightened as I saw just how worn and tired she looked, and how much had changed in the short time since she first greeted me when I came home. She only wanted to make me happy, so why...

"That won't happen."

She looked up, puzzled. "It won't? How do you – "

"You said that other side only comes out when you think I'm in danger, right? If that's true, I don't think she'd ever try to hurt me. She even saved me once."

"...At school?"

"Mhm – she took down the minotaur like it was nothing, and stopped it from hurting anyone else. Someone like that can't be all bad, right?"

"Then..." Lily gave a hesitant smile as she leaned forward. "Is it really ok to feel this way?"

My heart started racing one more as Lily brought her face even closer. Her eye, though ringed by a deep shadow and slightly puffy, shimmered with a tranquil passion I couldn't pull away from. Without thinking, I felt myself moving toward her as well.

"Yuu, I..."

The space between us lessened.

"Think I…"

Our lips hesitated on the slight gap between them, allowing for only one more word before they met.

"L– "

With a sudden gush of air, the bedroom door swung wide open, causing us to pull away, startled. Athena had returned with a wet cloth and roll of bandages, and was looking at us curiously.

"Oh, my apologies, did I interrupt? I can return later should it – "

"No, no, it's fine," I said, trying to hide my embarrassment by dragging myself back over to the bed.

"Ah, very well. I was hoping to clean out your wounds and rebandage them now."

She glanced at Lily, who still seemed to be in shock over the whole affair.

"Lily, could I ask for your help? I'm afraid it's much easier with an extra set of hands."

"Hm? I, um – " She stood up and took the cloth from Athena and nodded quickly. "I will."

Lily sat down on the side bed and held out her hand. "C-can I see your arm please?"

I scooched closer to her and did as she asked, placing my forearm in her palm.

"T-thank you."

She gingerly pulled at a loose piece of bandage, unraveling the wrappings and taking out the soiled gauze underneath. Athena had been insistent that we stock up on medical supplies which, although it seemed a little overly cautious at first, were remarkably handy to have around at a time like this.

As Lily removed last bit of cloth, I was finally able to get a good look at the bite marks. Even though they were a lot deeper than I expected, with a decent piece of flesh taken out where the creature's upper fangs had torn into, they looked like they were already starting to heal. None of us knew exactly why my injuries went away so quickly, but the most logical conclusion was that it had something to do with Lily's gift. Since even she wasn't sure exactly how it worked, it seemed easiest to just assume that part of the whole "not dying" thing included wounds and the like mending at a much faster rate.

"This might hurt a little, but I'll try to be quick."

Lily balled up the washcloth and pressed it softly against my skin, wiping carefully around the gashes. As I watched her meticulously work away, I couldn't help but appreciate how dexterous she really was. Lily nimbly wove her fingers around and between each wound, only causing me to wince a few times as she quickly cleaned them out. Before I knew it, she had done the same for my back, and was holding my hand as Athena bandaged up a fresh piece of gauze.

"And…there."

Athena patted down the last bit of adhesive and moved my arm in a circle.

"How does that feel?"

"Not bad, actually."

I turned my arm over, admiring their handiwork. Even though neither of them was human, they had plenty of finesse when it came to treating one.

"I'm sorry for causing you both so much trouble. I know I shouldn't be relying on you so much like this, so once I –"

Athena knocked me on the head softly, making me recoil. "Why do you say such foolish things? Are you not the one who claimed we are friends?"

"Yeah, but I – "

"Yuu." Lily took my face in her hands and looked at me with a tenderness that made me feel like I was the only person in her world. "It's ok to be weak. It's ok to be strong. And you don't have to be either. Just – be you."

"I – " I felt my own tears welling up, though I couldn't explain why. "Thank you…" I murmured, wiping away the few that had risen past on my sleeve, as Lily pulled me into her own tight embrace.

"Whatever differences we may possess, there is one thing uniform between us - " Athena smoothed out a spot next to Lily and sat down. "We shall always stand beside you."

"That's right," Lily said quietly. "If you really accept us for who we are, why wouldn't we do the same for you?"

Completely worn out both emotionally and physically, I only managed a single nod before drifting back to sleep in her arms.

13

"Date, date, date, going on a date~" Lily sang to herself, packing up her bag.

Since Lily and I had promised Himeo we'd help collect forms from the club leaders for the festival next week, the classroom had long been emptied out. By the time we finished tracking everyone down, the school was almost entirely vacant, save for those few student council members taking care of last-minute business.

"You ready to go?" I asked as I threw my backpack over my shoulder and took Lily's hand.

"Mhm mhm!" Lily pressed herself against my arm, giving me a sharp chill even through my jacket. "Where are we going again?"

"I was thinking we'd check out an arcade, maybe? There's one not too far from here, and I haven't been there in a while. I thought it might be fun to go together."

"Ohh – " Lily's eyes lit up with excitement. "I've never been to one before! I remember seeing it in a show once – there's a lot of lights and everything is all 'boom' and 'woosh' and 'skeplow', right?" She waved her hand in the air to emphasize each sound effect.

"Uh…yeah. Something like that."

"Then what are we waiting for? Let's go, let's go, let's go!"

I stumbled to catch up as Lily ran ahead, dragging me out the door.

A few days had passed since her fight with Athena, but I was relieved to see that she had already bounced back to her cheery, excitable self. Although neither of them appeared to hold any kind of grudge over what happened, I still felt guilty about causing the whole mess in the first place; that's why I figured the least I could do was take Lily out somewhere fun, and hopefully take her mind off things for a little. Even if she seemed ok on the surface, I had a feeling that those fears she exposed to us remained, tucked away in a place that'd take a while longer to reach.

Nevertheless, after a little bit of walking we soon found ourselves standing in front of the "FunZone GameCenter", an unrelenting and raucous symphony of sights and sounds awaiting inside. With a thousand different lights flashing and just as many alarms, bells, and whirs going off to match them, there was a hecticness to the place that, while exciting at first, could quickly become overwhelming if this wasn't your kind of thing.

Thankfully, Lily seemed to have lost none of her eagerness on the way over, and continued to tug me along.

Wandering outside the wide glass windows and doors that made up the front of the arcade were a number of girls clad in colorful outfits, some dressed like characters from popular games, and others in more "traditional" costumes, like a maid's dress or nurse's uniform. All of them were holding stacks of papers and pamphlets, handing out fliers for other game and hobby shops around the area, as well as coupons for the arcade itself. As soon as Lily noticed them, she came to a dead stop, transfixed by the display.

"See something you like?" I asked as a girl in an ornate black dress lined with light blue accents passed by.

"They're all so pretty!" Lily fidgeted dropped her gaze to the ground, adding quietly: "I wish I could look like that…"

"Then why don't we get you some clothes like that sometime?" I teased, heading towards the entrance.

"Really? You…you mean it?"

"I, uh – yeah. We'll figure something out."

I didn't think she'd take what I said so seriously, but there was no way I could just go and crush her dreams like that. I had no clue where you could get these kinds of costumes in the first place, but something told me Jun would be able to help with that. I made a mental note to ask him about it later.

"Yay, thank you thank you! You're the best~" Lily squeezed my hand as a hint of a blush rose in her pale cheeks. "But, you know, it'd make me even happier if I could wear something you liked…"

I gave an awkward laugh as I tried to shake off any impure thoughts her comment might imply. "Ah, well, you'd look great in anything. So as long as you're happy, I'm hap– "

I stopped short as I noticed, out of the corner of my eye, one of the promoters staring at us. I took a second look in her direction to see if it was someone I knew, maybe from school or around the neighborhood, and locked eyes with her – a petite girl with tan skin and short, brown hair. Coupled with a set of cat ears and tail, she had on a light blue tank top and white miniskirt which, while not as complex as some of the other outfits, did a lot to emphasize the "cute" aesthetic she had going. Still, she definitely wasn't anyone I recognized, so I quickly turned away and rushed inside.

"Is everything ok?" Lily asked as the dull rumble from outside became a full-blown cacophony of bleeps and bloops and calls for new challengers, forcing her to have to practically shout to be heard.

"Oh, yeah, it's nothing – I thought I saw someone staring at us, but it was probably just my imagination."

"Hmhmhm." Lily murmured, nudging me with her shoulder. "Maybe you've got a secret admirer?"

"Nah, that wouldn't happen."

"Why not?"

As always, Lily was entirely earnest in her line of questioning.

"I'm just…not really the kind of guy things like that happen to. It wasn't like she was someone I knew, and even if it was – I've already got you, don't I?"

Lily paused, thinking it over. "But what if someone else *did* like you?"

"Nothing, I guess. Like I said, I'm already dating you, silly."

"Yeah, but – " Lily let go of my hand and dashed ahead, blocking the path forward. "You said before loving someone means you want to make them happy, right?"

"Well, yeah, but that's only part – "

"So…" She smiled deviously and leaned forward. "If you love lots of people, and lots of people love you, then lots more people would be happy, right?"

"Sure, I mean that's one way to think about it, but – "

"But…?"

"For most people, being in love means committing to one person, and that person only."

Lily tilted her head to the side. "Why only one?"

"Ah, well, y'see…"

I struggled to come up with a decent explanation, but

everything felt like I was simply regurgitating what other people had already told me. If I was being honest, this wasn't the kind of question I had ever given serious thought before.

"I guess most people would say that you can only love someone if you focus all your feelings on that one person."

"But what would *you* say?" Lily stepped forward, bringing her face close to mine. "What if you love lots of people?"

"Then I'd have to choose the one I care about the most. So you, of course."

I wasn't necessarily opposed to the idea of loving multiple people, but this was the kind of subject best broached at another time, after I had the chance to think it through more. For now, that half-truth would have to suffice.

"Hmhmhm," Lily repeated, nodding to herself. "I don't know if that's fair to the other girls who love you, though," she added with an enigmatic smile.

"Wait, what do you mean other – ?"

Before I could finish my question, Lily ran off to a different part of the arcade, giggling to herself all the while and forcing me to chase after her. After zig-zagging through a few machines and squeezing past the other patrons milling about, I found her standing in front of one of the many crane machines littered throughout the arcade. This particular unit was filled white rabbits, their simple, black thread noses and red-bead eyes giving them a sort of patchwork look.

"You really like rabbits, huh?" I asked as I slipped a few coins into the machine.

"They're so fluffy…" Lily said without taking her eyes off the gaggle of stuffed toys.

"Here, why don't you try it out?" I repositioned Lily at the center of the controls and stood behind her.

"W-w-wait, how do you play?"

The crane jolted to life as Lily frantically looked from the panel in front of her to the stuffed rabbits.

"Don't worry, don't worry, I'll show you."

I placed my hand over hers and moved it to the joystick, holding back the inevitable and involuntary shivers.

"You use this to move it around –"

The claw began to swing wildly as we moved it across the play area.

"And when you've got it where you want it, press this to drop it down." I pointed to the flashing red button on her right as I took a step back. "And that's all there really is to it – she's all yours now."

Lily gave a determined nod and crouched down, skulking around each side of the machine as she tried to line up the perfect angle of attack. After a few minor adjustments, she at last seemed satisfied, pressed down on the button, and…

Nothing.

The claw lowered, limply tugged at a pile of bunnies, and fell on its side, ineffectually grasping at the air around it as it came back up.

"It didn't pick it up…" Lily whispered forlornly.

"Yeah, these things can be pretty hard to win," I said, hugging her gently. "Why don't I give it a try as well?"

I leaned down to put a few more coins in the machine. As the claw sprang to life again, I moved it over to what looked like a loose pile of rabbits and quickly tapped the button. The metal tendrils wrapped themselves around one of the lifeless prey beneath it, tugged tight, and brought it to the lip of the redemption slot –

Before letting it slip loose and tumble away.

"Er, just a bit of bad luck," I said with a half-hearted laugh. "Let me try again – "

And so it went on, and on, and on – the claw would pick up a plush, carry it right to the edge of the prize area, and then let it go at the very last second. Many a time I thought about how a wiser or more frugal man would call it quits then and there, would give up and cut their losses.

But not I.

Whether it was the courage of a warrior that Athena had instilled in me, or the fresh memory of Lily's pitiful expression burned into my mind, I could not – I *would* not – surrender. Man had created machine, and by god I would not lose to one as lowly as this. Coins and bills flowed from my pocket like a cascade of riches that would put to shame even the greatest of emperors, and in the end, what did I have to show for it?

A small, stuffed rabbit.

With a tired smile, I handed it over to Lily, her face beaming as she hugged it to her chest tight as could be. Needless to say, I had spent way more than what any reasonable person should have, but watching Lily snuggle up to her new friend was a sight worth more than any amount of money in the world.

"Why don't we take your new friend to see some of the other games here?"

Lily gave a swift nod but then – as if remembering something important – paused, stood up on her tiptoes, and gave me a light peck on the cheek.

"A little thank you for such a sweet gift," she said softly.

"Y-yeah, no problem" I mumbled, rubbing my cheek as I took Lily's free hand in my own.

As we wandered away from that part of the arcade, Lily keeping her rabbit safely tucked against her bosom, I couldn't help but share a little in her overwhelming jubilance. Although I had seen her smile plenty of times in the relatively short span she'd been here, she'd never looked quite so freely happy as she did now. With all that must've been weighing on her, I held on to the small hope that she was finally starting to let go of some of her insecurities, and feel like this was her home - a place where she could figure out (and be accepted for) who she really was.

"C'mon, c'mon, let's go!" Lily pulled me along to the next machine, undaunted in her quest to try every game she came across.

"Alright, alright, no need to rush."

I stood back and admired Lily as she fully invested herself in yet another shooting game, adroitly blasting away slavering hordes of zombies with a faded pink gun. It had been a while since I was able to truly put aside all the strange things happening around me as well and have some pure, unadulterated fun. Since there would always be time to worry about the future, and my place in it, I wanted to, if only for a day, forget the troubles that lay ahead and cherish this time with Lily – the goofy, innocent, earnest, sweet, excitable, gentle, protective, ever-curious girl I felt myself falling for more and more.

After a while longer of playing and patrolling, we finally reached the outer parts of the arcade, where Lily noticed a wall of yellow-trimmed doors.

"What's this?" she asked, running up to one and trying to peer through the small glass window on the front.

"These? I think they're karaoke rooms."

"Kary…oaky?"

"Yeah, you pick out a song and then sing along to it."

Lily's eye lit up once again at the mention of the word "sing".
"Can we try it? Please please please?"

Without waiting for a response, Lily dragged me over to the
clerk's desk and requested a room. Despite the fact that I sang
like a dying whale, there was no way I could say no to her.
Plus, it would at least be interesting to hear Lily's singing voice
(presuming spirits even had the same concept of singing as
humans in the first place).

After paying for our time and getting a key, we set ourselves
up in one of the booths near the end. The room itself was cozy,
with two red couches along the back and side, and a small,
round table placed in the center. Lily immediately plopped
down in the middle of the right-hand couch and opened up the
song book lying on the table, pouring over each page carefully.
I took a seat beside her and stretched out my legs – we had
been on our feet ever since getting here, so it felt nice to take a
load off.

"Ah! They have it!" Lily exclaimed, handing me the book
and pointing to her selection.

"Huh, I'm kind of surprised you know any songs from this
world," I said as I punched the appropriate number into the
keypad.

"Oh, I…I heard it a few years ago."

A moment later and the screen lit up, a series of forests,
waterfalls, and mountains fading past as a slow, melodic tune
drifted from the speakers. It wasn't a song I recognized, but it
was certainly a pretty one regardless – the music was relaxing,
with enough instrumentation to even be a little moving. Lily
turned her attention to the screen, and as the first words
popped up, she began to sing.

When the nights, are long

And the sky is missing stars
All alone, I'll walk
Just to be there by your side

She was good.

She was *really* good.

Her singing was soft, but with a depth and profound sense of emotion that set it apart from anything I had ever heard before. Each note felt like it resonated in my heart, and carried with it the muted passion of some unknown longing.

When the days, are gone
And twilight takes you hand
All alone, I'll walk
Just to see you by my side

I watched Lily intently, totally absorbed by her performance. It felt like it was reaching out to me on a level I didn't even understand myself.

…

Was this the kind of power spirits had over mortals?

If the time, does come
When we have to go our way
I'll hold, on tight
To my nothing just the same

As Lily finished singing, she placed the microphone back on the table and turned to me, slightly embarrassed.

"What did you think?"

"You – you were amazing, I had no idea you could sing like that! Or, uh, anyone, for that matter."

Lily smiled meekly and squirmed in her seat, tugging at the hem of her shirt. "You don't have to be so nice…"

"No, no, I'm being honest, really! You were nothing short of astounding. Who taught you to sing like that?"

"I…never really learned. That's the only song I know."

Lily gave a small laugh as she picked up the song book and began to flip it through again. It was easy to tell that this was somewhat of a sore spot for her, so I tried my best to keep the conversation moving along.

"Then…do you like singing? I think this was the first time I've ever heard you do it."

Lily smiled again – a much warmer, more natural smile than before. "Whenever I was lonely, I would hum that song to myself. I never even knew the words, just the melody." She had wistful look in her eye, as if looking back on another time and place. "Although maybe what I said before wasn't entirely true. I did learn that song from someone…very special."

"Oh? Another spirit?"

Lily shook her head. "No, he was a human. He died a couple years ago - I-I don't know how many - but I remember how he would sing to himself when he was alone, too. Even if he didn't know I was there, I always enjoyed listening." She inched herself closer and tentatively moved one finger over mine. "I think it'd make him happy to know you liked it so much."

"Yeah, I…I think so too."

Even if I didn't know the full story, I understood the weight of Lily's words. Her relationship with the human world was one of fascination, curiosity, longing, and – though I could only speculate at this point – shame. The task she carried out was undeniably a beneficial and necessary one, but I couldn't imagine that she ever had much of a chance to see the brighter side of humanity, if all she was ever greeted with were grieving families and their recently departed. With this small, seemingly innocuous confession, I started to better see how she viewed the world we now both lived in.

Fortunately, Lily being Lily, she wasn't one to let things stay heavy for long, and before I knew it we were both laughing and joking together once more. Despite my initial protests, she had effortlessly guilted me into singing, with fairly predictable results. My low notes were flat, my high notes could shatter glass, and none of it seemed to make a difference to her – Lily only smiled and clapped along with each violent rendition, cheering me on throughout. The next hour flew by as we took turns on the microphone, even dabbling in a few duets together (which she mercifully took the lead on).

Both our voices and feet thoroughly worn out, we finally decided to return home once our rental time was up. Lily continued to clutch to her rabbit as we exited the arcade, having not let it out of her grasp for even a second since I gave it to her.

I pulled my jacket tighter around my shoulders, trying to brace myself against the frigid winds billowing past. It looked like most of the promoters had already gone home, as a stream of pedestrians likewise leaving work took their place. As me and Lily moved past the flow of people going further into the city, I felt a somehow-familiar presence following us. I turned my head back to confirm my suspicions, and - sure enough – the same girl staring at us earlier was standing nearby, watching closely.

Lily followed my gaze and, taking notice of the strange girl as well, gave me a puzzled look, which I could only answer with an equally-confused shrug. I was debating whether I should go over and ask if she was okay, or if I knew her from somewhere else and somehow forgot, when I heard a terse voice rise from the crowd.

"So this is where you've been all along?"

At first I thought that this odd statement might've been addressed to me, but I was able to see that the speaker was talking to the girl with cat ears. He was a reasonably tall man, somewhere around 6 and a half feet, wearing a suit made entirely of varying shades of white. It wasn't unusual to see people in business attire all over the city, especially once the work day came to an end, but, be it his unique choice of color coordination or the harsh tone of his voice, there was something…off about him.

As the man in white loomed over the girl, he grabbed ahold of her wrist with one hand while punctuating his words with the other. However, since he seemed to be talking in a more hushed tone now, I couldn't quite make out what he was saying. The girl, in turn, only stared at the ground, a blank expression on her face as she mutely nodded along.

"Should we do something?" Lily whispered.

"Yeah, I – I'll go talk to them."

I forced myself to walk towards the pair, my body numb and my mind blank – what exactly was I trying to accomplish?

"E-excuse me," I mumbled, trying to steady my voice as I stepped in front of the white-suited man. He immediately turned his attention to me with a sharp glare, his eyes a misty grey and his mouth contorted into a strained neutrality.

"What do you want?" he asked with a dry, hoarse voice.

It took all my effort not to blurt out "I have no idea" right then and there.

"Oh, um, I was just…"

C'mon, think, *think*.

The man gave a wry smile as he stood up straight, yanking the girl to his side. "It's very rude to interrupt those you have no business with, young man. I suggest you be on your way.

Now."

The tenor of his words left little interpretation as to how much of a "suggestion" this really was.

The girl glanced from the man to me with wide, frightened eyes, her body trembling as she began to shuffle away, following the man's lead. Even if I didn't know what was going on, I knew I had to do something – *anything* – before they got away.

"Wait, wait!" I shouted, running after the two.

The man in white stopped in his tracks and slowly turned around. "What is it now? We have no business together, so I ask that you no longer pester – "

"I was…I was just wondering what you were doing with my roommate."

"Room. Mate?" The man let each word drip from his tongue like venom.

"Er – yeah, she's been working at this arcade for a while now, so I come to pick her up every day."

"T-that's right!" Lily added, moving beside me. "She didn't say anything about someone else coming to get her today. Are you a friend of hers?" Despite the blatant lie, Lily managed to maintain a perfect façade of earnest concern.

"I suppose you could say I am her guardian – though that should be of no concern to either of you. My dear kitty simply seemed to have lost her way, and now we must return home posthaste." The man gave a curt nod and turned around to leave once more.

"Hey!"

I shouted out to the girl, who looked back, surprised. I had noticed she was wearing a sort of necklace, a thin silver chain with a small pendant in the center. As it jangled to the side, I could just barely make out a name inscribed on it – Nina.

"Um, Nina, do you actually know this guy?"

The girl paused and, looking from the man to us, took a step forward. "I, um, I mean, y-ye–" She had a light and airy, almost childish, voice.

"How do you know her name?" the man interrupted, finally letting go of the girl as he stepped in front of her.

"Like I said, she's our roommate. She's been living with us for at least a few months, so you must have the wrong person. Right Nina?"

The girl scurried out from behind the man and nodded vigorously. "R-right."

"I'd be happy to help you look for your friend, if she's still missing – "

"Don't you dare mock me," the man said with a quiet intensity, bending down to bring his face close to mine. "I've no idea what you are planning, but if you do not quit these ridiculous games, I will have no choice but to – "

"Ah–ah, I'd hold off on that. It'd probably be a bad idea to make a big scene with all these people around."

Sure enough, a few bystanders had already begun to gather around, wondering what was going on.

The man glanced from side to side, then stood back up, a satisfied grin on his face. "Perhaps you are correct. I must have been mistaken. My apologies." As he took a step back and was swallowed up by the crowd behind him, his final words echoed in my mind. "Know this – the burden you have chosen to inherit is of your own doing. There is, after all, no such thing as coincidences."

"Yuu? Are you ok?" Lily grabbed my shoulder and shook me gently, snapping me back to reality.

"Oh, yeah, I'm fine. I – "

I looked to the girl standing beside Lily, who was now holding on to shirt sleeve, her gaze fixed on the spot where that man had faded out of sight. Her hair was slightly unkempt, and her clothes a little soiled here and there, but she otherwise looked no worse for wear.

"I'm, uh, sorry about what happened back there," I said, kneeling down. She was a bit shorter than both me and Lily, so I felt like I should at least try to talk with her eye-to-eye. "I didn't mean to get involved, but it looked like he was trying to take you away. I – I hope I didn't make a mistake or anythi– "

Before I could finish speaking, the girl threw her arms around my neck and fell into me. "Thank you thank you thank you! I don't know who you are Mr. Stranger but you saved Nina!"

The girl was now full of energy and vigor, a total 180 from how quiet and reticent she appeared before.

"Nina saw you go by earlier and knew you were a good person. She can tell things like that." The girl – who it seems I could fairly assume was, in fact, named Nina – pulled her face away and beamed with pride.

"I'm, uh, glad we could help," I said, somewhat baffled at this spontaneous affection. "Who was that guy, anyway?"

Nina furrowed her brow as her voice became low. "Gregory. His name is Gregory. He was Nina's master, ever since she was little. Nina tried to escape, but he found her again."

She perked up as a new realization dawned on her.

"But now he's gone! And since you saved Nina, Nina needs to thank you!"

"Oh, no, there's no need, really," I said, backing up. I looked to Lily for help, but she only giggled and nudged me forward, having fun with the whole situation.

"But Nina can do lots of things! She can cook, clean, do the laundry, she – " Nina paused, her mouth agape. "She can come live with you!"

"…Come again?"

"Nina can be really useful, she'll show you! And – " She stood on her tip-toes, eyes sparkling. "And you can be Nina's new master!"

"No, no, really, that's alright, you don't have to do anything like that – "

"But we'd be happy to have you regardless. Right, Yuu?" Lily reached out to and patted Nina on the head, who smiled and wriggled in place.

"I mean, it's true that we have plenty of space, but don't you have some place you need to go back to?"

Nina tilted her head curiously.

"Like your home?"

"Nina…doesn't have a home, mister," she said softly.

"Then you're not from around here, I take it?"

She shook her head. "Nina's never been to this place before. A few months ago Nina's master started acting really weird, so she knew she had to get away. She tried to find some way out of his house, but she only found this big, glowing rock. The next thing she knew, Nina was in this strange place she'd never ever seen. She got scared and ran away, but some nice people found here."

She tugged on the bottom of her tank top and smiled to herself.

"When she told them she didn't have a home, they gave her these clothes and said she could stay in that building at night. All she had to do was stand out here and be nice to people."

Everything was starting to come together: a random girl

showing up in a place she'd never seen before, her odd mannerisms, the weird guy following her – this had to be another spirit.

"Then I…guess I can't exactly leave you here by yourself. If you really want, you're welcome to come stay with us, at least until we find you a more permanent place."

"Really? You mean it?"

"Yeah, as long as you're ok with it."

"Yes, yes, yes!" Nina clung to my arm, bouncing up and down. "Mas-ter, mas-ter, new mas-ter~"

"J-just Yuu is fine," I muttered, feeling my cheeks flare up. "Anyway, it'll be dark soon so we should start heading home."

"Home…" Nina repeated the word, letting it linger on her lips.

"You'll love it there," Lily said, taking Nina's other hand. "There's a big tv, and a really pretty garden, and a super comfy bed – plus, Yuu's a great cook so he'll make you whatever you like!"

"That might be overstating it a bit," I said sheepishly.

"That's ok! Nina knows how to cook lots and lots and lots of things, so she'll take care of that from now on!" She puffed out her chest proudly.

"That's amazing!" Lily said. "I've always wanted to learn – maybe you can teach me?"

"Yes, yes! Nina will show, um…"

"Lily," she said with a smile.

"Lily how to be the best cooker ever!"

"I look forward to it," Lily said with a giggle, as the three of us followed the street lights home, one after another coming to life against the encroaching twilight.

14

"Heya, we're home," I called out, opening the door. "I've got a lot to tell you, so I hope – "

I cut myself off as I found a very long, very sharp sword leveled at my neck.

"Uh, Athnena? What – "

"Step aside," she interrupted coldly. "It would appear that a stray has taken to following you home."

"You don't mean – "

I glanced behind me at Nina, who had grabbed on to the back of my jacket and was peeking out from the side.

"Oh no, no, you've got it all wrong. This is Nina – we saw some guy trying to take her away, so me and Lily stepped in to try and help. Since she doesn't have anywhere else to go, I offered to let her stay with us for a while."

Athena lowered her weapon slightly, though her arm was still tense, fingers tightly curled around the grip. "Do you know what she is?"

"A...girl?" I ventured cautiously.

Athena shook her head. "She is a monster, a creature not born of this world. As she has no place in this realm, let alone this home, allow me to finish thi– "

"Hey, hey, hey!" I threw out my arms, blocking Athena's path.

"What do you think you're doing?"

"Was I not clear? This creature is neither mortal nor spirit, and must be dealt with accordingly."

I looked back at Nina once more, who hadn't budged from her spot. "Wait, you're not a spirit?"

"No!" she proclaimed defiantly. "I'm a kitty – see?" She shook her head and swished her tail to demonstrate.

"Then...that's not a costume?"

"Mm mm! They're really real, master – look, look!" She grabbed my hand and placed it behind one of her ears, which twitched in response to my touch.

"Do you see now?" Athena asked, a hint of annoyance in her voice. "Though they are somewhat of a rarity, monstrous half-beasts such as this do, indeed, exist."

I placed a hand on Athena's sword, pushing it down. "Ok, but why do you have your weapon out? She hasn't even done anything – "

"*Yet.* There is no telling what these creatures are capable of, and so in the interest of not only your own well-being, but that of all the mortals who inhabit this realm, I must insist we remain resolute in our efforts." She looked past me, to Lily now. "You must share in this sentiment as well, do you not?"

"I...I don't see why she can't live here," Lily said softly. "Whether she's a monster or not, she seems harmless enough, and she still needs a home either way."

"That's right!" Nina cut in, still half-hiding behind me. "Master said that Nina could live here, and so she's not leaving his side! Never ever ever!"

Athena raised one eyebrow and looked back at me, perplexed. "Master?"

"I...have no idea myself, I'm just kind of going along with it for now."

With that, Athena seemed to finally relent, sheathing her blade and letting out an extended sigh. "I see there is no use is prolonging this argument. At least come in from the cold, then we may discuss this in greater detail."

I happily closed the door behind us and ushered Nina in. Things were certainly more contentious than I'd expected, but I was sure I could win Athena over once I explained the situation. It might just take a little more…roundabout convincing.

"Hey, Lily – could you take Nina upstairs and give her a bath first? That should help warm her up a little."

"Oh, yeah, of course!" Lily grabbed Nina's hand and started to lead her away. "You can borrow some of my clothes once you're all cleaned up – they might be a little loose, but it'll be good for you to get changed into something else."

"O-oh, ok," Nina said quietly, following close behind. Despite her initial enthusiasm, it was plain to see that it would take a little time for her to get used to being in a new home. Still, this afforded me the exact opportunity I was looking for.

"She's a nice girl, y'know," I said once Nina and Lily made their way up to the second floor. "I don't know the whole story, but it sounds like she's had it pretty rough."

"Mm." Athena had taken a seat at the kitchen table and was staring off into the distance.

"The way Nina explained it, she was more or less a servant since she was born. Had to serve some guy in another world her whole life." I turned on the stove to let some water boil and placed a few mugs on the counter.

"I see no reason why that should concern me."

"Do you really think that?"

I took a chair opposite Athena, looking directly at her. She tilted her head in my direction and frowned. "What might you be implying?"

"This doesn't seem like you. One of the first things you said when we met was that you were a protector of the innocent, a defender of the weak, a guiding li– "

"And she is neither of those things." She placed her hands on the table and leaned forward, dropping her voice low. "Do you take my values for childish naivete? Do you know of the inherent nature of those creatures? They are mindless beasts, deceptively vicious and endlessly destructive, with little to redeem their meager existence."

"Why would you say something like that? You saw how scared she was just coming here, there's no reason for you to threaten her or – "

"Tell me yourself – was the minotaur who gored you reasonable? Were those wolves you slew kind and merciful?"

"I mean, no, but that's hardly – "

"I can forgive your ignorance, given you have not seen the savagery creatures such as her are so easily capable. But in this matter you must believe me."

Athena's eyes were clear and focused, filled with neither hate nor fear - only an unwavering conviction which I could not fully grasp.

"To allow her to remain here is to invite disaster. Though it may seem harsh, we must be both preemptive and swift in our protection of this world."

"I won't deny that I'm inexperienced, especially compared to you," I said slowly, doling out each word with care. "And I do trust you when you say you're only trying to look out for me. But there's one thing I don't think you've fully considered."

"And what might that be?"

"This is your chance to do more than just eradicate evil – you can reform it."

"...What are you suggesting?"

The kettle began to whistle, forcing me to jump up and attend to it. "Nothing, really. I'm only saying that if you think all monsters are inherently bad, you can do more by showing them a better way, instead of just killing them or sending them back to their own world."

Grabbing hold of the kettle's handle with a rag, I poured some water into the four mismatched mugs waiting to the side.

"Maybe the creatures we fought before were more feral, or impossible to reach out to, but Nina doesn't seem even close to anything like that."

Athena said nothing for a moment, mulling over what I said.

"And what if it is all an act?"

I returned to my seat and handed Athena a cup, along with a packet of tea. Contrary to my initial expectations, she much preferred the sweeter blends and always insisted on adding honey, to the point that it had quickly become a regular item on my shopping list.

"Then I'll take responsibility for her. Although, if anything, I think what she needs most is a big sister to serve as her role model. Y'know, someone to show her right from wrong, set her on the right path."

I pretended to busy myself with my own tea packet, watching Athena's reaction out of the corner of my eye.

"W-well, I-I suppose it would not hurt to try..." She stared down at the table with flushed cheeks, trying to hide her smile.

"Great, then it's decided!"

"H-hold on, I said no such thing – !"

196

"Hey, sorry for the wait," Lily said, rounding the corner and shaking her head. Her hair was still wet and hung straight down, though she used what semblance of bangs she could comb over to the right to cover her eye. "Nina insisted I take a bath with her, so it took a little longer than I expected. What'd we miss?"

Both of the girls had changed into flannel pajamas, although, just as Lily predicted, they hung loose over Nina's small frame, causing her to look more like a child dressing up as an adult, than…whatever age she actually was. Nevertheless, Nina shuffled over to the seat next to me, pant legs dragging on the ground, and scooted her chair closer, grabbing onto my arm once more.

"Ah, Athena was just saying that, given everything that's happened, she'd be happy to let Nina stay with us. Right?"

Athena shot me a piercing glare that more or less confirmed I'd be paying for this during training tomorrow.

"Yes, for now," she muttered into her mug. "Although I should warn you – your utmost respect and servility will be expected at all times. No transgression will go unaccounted for, no mistake disavowed. You will need to show not only your utility in this home, but that you can reign in that natural and bestial nature, therefore – "

"Master?" Nina whispered, tugging on my sleeve. "What's she talking about?"

"Um…" I hesitated, knowing I shouldn't translate exactly what Athena said. "She's just saying that you should be a good girl, and be on your best behavior."

"Oh! Nina always does that!" She nodded to herself sagely, as Lily tried to stifle her own giggles.

"…Have either of you been paying attention at all?" Athena

asked coldly.

"Hm? Yeah, totally – but before I forget, I should introduce you both properly." I pointed to Lily and Athena in turn. "You already know Lily – she's my girlfriend. And that's Athena, who I guess you could call my teacher. They're both spirits, so neither of them are from this world, just like you."

Nina's ears perked up at the mention of "spirits", her eyes shimmering with excitement. "So that's what Nina felt! She knew if you were friends with a spirit, you had to be a good human." She squeezed herself against my arm, smiling contentedly. "Nina can tell these kinda things, y'know."

"Then that would explain why you were staring at us…" I murmured to myself, handing the girls the remaining drinks.

"But how did you know I was a spirit in the first place?" Lily asked.

"These…hybrids, as they are called," Athena cut in, "are all able to - varying degrees - detect the presence of spirits. It is no surprise that she could not only sense your true nature, but Yuu's connection to us." Athena paused, eyeing me carefully. "You do understand her potential, correct?"

I thought it over for a second. "With that sort of power, we could track down any wayward spirits much faster, rather than just hoping we bump into them."

"Good, good. I'm happy to see you're learning more than simply how to swing a sword. Tactics are what truly allow one to – "

"There's one problem, though," I interrupted. "That's not why she's with us. If Nina wants to help out in that way, that's great, but she's our guest first and foremost. The decision remains hers."

Nina closed her eyes and furrowed her brow, tilting her head side to side. "Nina doesn't really understand, but if she can help master too, then she'll do it. She'll…she'll show you how useful she can be!"

I laughed and ruffled her hair a bit, its silky texture unlike anything I'd ever felt before. "If you're sure you're up for it, that'd be a big help."

Nina balled her fists and gave a firm nod. "Master just needs to leave it to Nina. She'll find all the spirits, wherever they're hiding."

The earnest determination, innocent curiosity, immediate affection – it already felt like having a second Lily around, albeit more in the vein of a little sister than romantic partner.

"Putting all that aside for now," Lily said, "why don't you tell us more about yourself? Like, what world did you come from?"

Nina hid her face against my arm, tightening her grip on my sleeve. "Nina…doesn't really know. All she can remember is living in a big house with her momma and Gregory ever since she was little."

"That was the guy trying to take her away," I clarified for Athena.

"Even though Nina lived with her momma, it was really lonely. She wasn't allowed to go outside, and Ruby was the only one who would ever come to visit."

"Ruby?" Lily asked.

"Mhm! She's Nina's best friend. But…" Nina hesitated, her voice quieting as she pulled herself closer. "One day, both of them went away. She waited and waited for them to come back, but they never did. But Nina knows they're still somewhere out there, looking for her! They…they have to be."

"Y-yeah, I'm sure they are," I said with as much conviction

as I could muster.

"But then why were you still living with that man?" Lily asked.

"Unfortunate though it is," Athena interjected again, "both affluent mages and spirits have been known to keep hybrids as pets. I imagine that such was the case for her and her mother."

"Is that true?"

Nina nodded slowly. "Even though Nina's old master never hurt her, he wouldn't let her go far from the house, and he…he said if she ever tried to leave, Nina would disappear for good. So she was a good kitty and always stayed inside, but – but – "

I could hear the tears rising up in her voice, and gently wrapped my arm around her head.

"It's ok, it's ok. He's gone now. You won't ever have to worry about him again."

I didn't know where this was coming from, but it felt like the right thing to say.

"R-really?"

Lily walked over to where we were sitting and stroked Nina's head. "Really really. We'll take care of you from now on."

"Y-you mean it?"

I glanced at Athena, suggesting it was her turn.

"Er, yes, so long as you find your accommodations satisfactory, then I'm sure you are welcome to stay as long as you'd like."

At last, the tears came rolling out.

"You're all…so nice…to Nina," she said between sobs. "She's…not…good enough – "

"No, no, don't say that," Lily cooed, embracing Nina from the other side. "Yuu told me something really important the other day."

"W-what?"

"You don't have to be good, you just have to be yourself. You can do that, right?"

"Nina…c-can."

Lily smiled warmly and touched her forehead to Nina's. "Then that's all you need to do. For as long as you want it to be, this is your home now."

"Then…do you think if Nina came here…Nina's momma might be, too?"

"I don't see why not," I said with a gentle smile.

"A-and Ruby, too?"

"The probability of such an event – " Lily shot Athena a harsh look as soon as she started. "Though low, does not make it impossible. We…will do our best to find them."

"Thank you, thank you, thank you," Nina whispered into my arm. "Nina's home…"

* * *

"Bedtime with master!" Nina exclaimed, overjoyed. After that bit of emotional catharsis, she had quickly regained her cheery affect and was a bundle of energy once more. In a single bound she had launched herself from the doorway and onto my bed, as me, Lily, and Athena attempted to fix up the sheets.

"Uh, Nina? You can have your own bed, you know?"

I was starting to notice an unfortunate pattern developing.

Nina crawled to the end of the bed and shook her head. "No no no! Nina said she would stay by master's side, and she always keeps her word."

"Sound familiar?" Lily teased, as Athena turned her head away in a huff.

"I – "

I let sighed and patted Nina on the head. I couldn't say no to a face like that.

"Fine. It might be a little crowded though." With Lily always on my right, and Athena on my left, there wasn't a whole lot of room left.

"Oh that's ok! Nina will just sleep on top of you, silly." She bounced on the bed a few times, giggling to herself. "She's really, really light, so she won't squish you."

"If you insist…" I murmured, as Lily threw her arms around me from behind and kissed my cheek, and Athena curtly insisted we all get to bed, given how late it already was.

In the end, all I could do was resign myself to the luckiest misfortune I'd ever found.

CPSIA information can be obtained
at www.ICGtesting.com
Printed in the USA
LVHW111108040119
602254LV00030B/13/P

9 780578 428918